Captive, Mine

Natasha Knight

Trent Evans

Copyright © 2015 by Natasha Knight and Trent Evans
All rights reserved.

Cover Design by Rachel A Olson
(www.nosweatgraphics.weebly.com)

This book is a work of fiction. The characters, incidents and dialogues are products of the author's imagination and as such, any similarity to existing persons, places or events must be considered purely coincidental.

This book contains content that is not suitable for readers aged 17 and under.

For mature readers only.

Published in the United States by Shadow Moon Press, Washington.

ISBN: 1508683808
ISBN-13: 978-1508683803

Manufactured in the United States of America

First Shadow Moon Press Electronic Edition: February 2015

BY TRENT EVANS

Published by Shadow Moon Press
A Message of Love

Maintenance Night

What She's Looking For

The Chronicles of Muurland Series:

The Fall of Lady Westwood

The Dominion Trust Series:

Becoming Theirs

Her Troika — The Complete Story

Expecting Surrender

Published By Stormy Night Publications
The Doctor and The Naughty Girl

What The Doctor Ordered

BY NATASHA KNIGHT

Published by Stormy Night Publications

Taught To Kneel

Taming Emma

Captive's Desire

Aching To Submit

Her Rogue Knight

Taken By The Beast

Claimed By The Beast

Taming Megan

Dangerous Defiance

The Firefighter's Girl

Taming Naia

Given To The Savage

Amy's Strict Doctor

Protective Custody

<u>Collections</u>

What The Doctor Ordered

Published by Cobblestone Press

Pierced

Other Collections

Sci Spanks 2014: A Collection of Spanking Science Fiction Romance Stories (Seasonal Spankings)

The Disciplinarian: A Collection of Short Spanking Stories

PROLOGUE

I always knew I was different. Knew I lived a different sort of life. I just didn't expect to end up here — like this.

For weeks I'd felt it. I'd known someone had been watching me. But I'd ignored it.

Looking back, I could think of a hundred ways I could have avoided this, avoided *him*. He'd said one thing and, like a fool, I had believed him. Useless words. Stolen words.

Tucking my knees into my chest, I pulled the worn blanket up over my body. He'd stripped me bare before bringing me here, before binding my wrists together so tightly they felt raw. I shivered in the cold, damp room knowing he was going to teach me a lesson. I'd been to this room before. I knew what had to happen here.

Tears again, stupid tears. He had no right to keep me captive. His captive.

"Let me out!" I screamed for the hundredth time, my voice hoarse, my throat too dry.

This time, though, there was an answer: the sound of his footsteps approaching, the almost imperceptible sound of the key sliding into the lock, turning it.

I pressed my back harder into the wall, fisting the blanket with sweaty hands.

I was going to be punished and it was going to be bad. I knew it. He'd promised it and he always kept his promises.

CHAPTER 1

It had happened, the cops had finally caught up with him.

Emanuel J. Cross, drug dealer to the wealthy, privileged addicts of high society, my father, had been arrested. And that wasn't the worst of it.

"Christ!" I said, watching the spectacle on TV. Daddy in handcuffs, walking between two men, the entire block cordoned off, reporters pouring over the yellow police tape to get a close-up of him in this, his grandest hour.

But they didn't know the half of it.

"Ma'am, we need to go."

I turned to the door. "Get out," I snapped. I wasn't even going to try to be sweet. My father had arranged things neatly for himself, and, apparently, for me. The arrest would be very public, we knew that. Couldn't exactly take one half of the two-man force that kept the entirety of the East Coast supplied with their drug of choice without some noise. But I found out yesterday that Daddy had made a deal with the feds months ago when they'd first caught up with him. Testify against Randall, his business partner and the one they wanted badly enough to make a deal with the likes of my father, enter into the Witness Protection Program, and live out his days in quiet suburbia in the middle of nowhere. Become a nobody. It was a different sort of prison really. Although I suppose federal prison would be worse. But what I was most pissed about was that I, too, had been given fifteen minutes to pack my essentials and leave my New York City apartment — my beloved apartment — with exactly one suitcase, and disappear right along with my father!

Yes, of course I understood what could happen to me if I was to refuse protection. Randall would do anything he could to keep my father quiet, and what surer way than through his one weakness: me.

"Ma'am." The man ducked his head into my room again and it took all I had not to kick the door shut right on his stubby, red nose.

"How do you expect me to pack up my life in fifteen minutes? Get out!" I turned my back on him.

"That's no way to speak to the officer, Ms. Cross."

I stilled instantly, a chill running along my spine.

"I got this. We'll be ready to go in one minute," the same man said.

I faced him as he closed my bedroom door.

I have to admit, it took me a minute to recover myself. This guy was tall. I'm not short, just average at 5'5", so he must have been 6'5" at least, with dark hair and darker eyes, eyes that made me pause. Under any other circumstances, I would have reacted differently, but not today. Not when my life was falling apart around me.

I cleared my throat. "Who the hell are you?"

He smiled and made no secret of looking me over from head to toe. I narrowed my eyes and did the same. At this point, most men would have tripped over themselves with some stupid comment, but *he* didn't. Instead, when I met his gaze again, he looked at me straight on, one side of his mouth curling upwards into a tiny smirk.

"I'm Lake Freeman. Your father hired me to look after you. I'll be your personal bodyguard until we get you settled and safe."

"I don't need a personal bodyguard," I said, my tone ice. "In case you hadn't noticed, I've got a room full of assholes out there who think they're my personal bodyguards."

"I'd appreciate if you could watch your language, Ms. Cross. It's no way for a young lady to speak."

My mouth fell open. I had no comeback. Really, he was offended by my language?

Lake glanced at the half-packed suitcase on the bed and walked over to it, his boots heavy on the hardwood floor. He pushed the lid down and zipped it up.

"Hey, I wasn't done packing." I took a step toward it, realizing I still held a blouse in my hand.

"Yes, you were," he said, his tone final.

I reached to unzip it but he grabbed hold of my wrist. And he wasn't gentle. "Get your hands off me! What do you think you're doing?"

"I'm saving your ass, princess," he said, his expression deadly serious. He picked up the suitcase while keeping hold of my wrist. "Let's go."

"Just a minute," I protested, pulling back.

He paused and turned toward me, making a show of checking his watch.

"How do I know you work for my father anyway?"

"Good girl," he said, releasing my wrist and smiling. "He said you might ask. It's Velveteen Rabbit, your safe code."

I stared at him. How long had it been since I'd heard my dad read me that story?

My mom had run out on us when I wasn't even a year old. I had no memory of her. My dad and I had been close all my life, so with all this crap that was happening, as tough as I tried to act, I was scared. I was scared for him and for me. And I guess he and I both knew all along that something like this could happen.

Ever since I was little, my dad and I had a secret code and that was it: The Velveteen Rabbit. It was my favorite book. He'd read it to me every night for a year and I still had my well-worn copy of it. I knew if ever someone said they'd been sent by my dad, they'd know those words. It hadn't come up before, and I didn't expect it to at twenty-four years old either. But there it was. My dad was still taking care of me from wherever he happened to be at the moment.

"We have to go," Lake said, this time he sounded almost nice.

I nodded once and looked away. I didn't want him to see the tears in my eyes and I didn't want him to know I was scared.

* * *

The pictures didn't do her justice. Not one bit.

He'd memorized them, of course, until he knew every line of her delicate face, the large brown eyes, the long, wavy black hair, the rich olive tone of her skin. He remembered lingering over the shot taken of her outside on the front stoop of her brownstone, the steam wafting up from her coffee in the chill morning air. The low angle of the morning light seemed to render the white gown she wore diaphanous, revealing far more of her figure than he knew she'd have liked.

He'd taken special care to memorize that photo.

Now, as the truck bounced over the pothole-ridden streets of the city, he watched her again. It made her uneasy, his gaze upon her. He found he liked that. Her eyes, like doe's eyes, darted to him frequently, as if by keeping him in her sight she was reassuring herself all was well.

It certainly wasn't, but she didn't need to know that. Not yet, anyway.

"You forgot something," he said, nodding toward her.

"Probably forgot all kinds of things." She glared at him, her eyes squinting against the sunshine pouring through the windshield. "Which wouldn't have been an issue had you let me, I don't know, *pack*."

Ah, yes, beautiful she may be — but that mouth.

"Try again, Ms. Cross."

She looked out the window, jabbing a thumb at the unmarked in the next lane. "We certainly didn't forget them. Like a goddamned motorcade. Very subtle."

"Seat belt."

"What?" Her hand reached up automatically for it, then she stopped herself. "You're serious with this?"

"Put it on."

Those big brown eyes stared back, her jaw tight. One of the tires dropped into a pothole large enough to swallow a man, her breasts moving with the jarring bounce of the truck. She winced, cursing under her breath, her gaze sliding away.

It was shaping up to be a long trip.

"Seatbelt, Ms. Cross."

"Are you my bodyguard, or my dad?"

He scanned ahead for an open stretch of curb, finding a loading zone for a busy restaurant supply business. It would do.

"What are you doing?"

Lake pulled the truck to the curb, the cruisers slowing to a crawl as horns blared from the cars behind them. One of the cruisers flashed his blues, waving the cars around him even as his puzzled white face peered over at their truck.

"Let's get this out of the way now." He leaned over her, and she shrank into the seat, her lips a surprised O. "I'm here to keep you *safe*, to get you to your new home." His hand caught the belt, whipping it out and around, seating the latch with a loud click. She inhaled sharply as he pulled up, cinching it tight, the shoulder belt snug between her breasts. "And I can't very well keep you safe if you die in a car wreck, can I?"

"I don't wear—"

"You didn't before, but you do now, Ms. Cross. This is a new life, a new start." He flashed her a grin, then pulled back onto the road, squeezing the big pickup between the two waiting cruisers.

"I can't believe this. This is a fucking nightmare." She flashed him a withering look. "I don't care what you think, Mr...whoever you are."

"Lake."

She frowned. "*Lake,* then. I don't wear seat belts."

"Never too late to start doing the right thing."

You could try taking your own advice, for once.

But it was much too late for that. Much too late for anything at all.

His earpiece crackled to life. "Everything okay in there?"

Tucking the cord fully behind his ear, he smiled over at the cruiser next to them. "We're good."

The detail had insisted on the radio, though he detested it, knowing how easy it was to pick up a signal from outside. It was pointless, and sloppy, but he needed to play nice for now. The two officers were more of a help than a hindrance at this point anyway, especially in getting them through the god-awful upper Manhattan traffic. Once they'd gotten closer to their destination, he'd have more options, wouldn't be so penned in. But that was still many hours away.

He glanced back over at her. She'd crossed her arms over those little jiggling breasts of hers, her head turned away. "Did the officers brief you on what's going to happen today?"

"They did all that at the sentencing for Daddy," she muttered, still looking out the window. "Said I wouldn't know when they were coming, but when they did, I'd have minutes to pack up. They never said anything about you though."

"Your father added that little detail at the last minute when there were...developments."

Her brown eyes turned to him then. "Developments?"

Traffic came to a standstill, the distant sound of horns blaring somewhere up ahead. He sighed, drumming fingers on the steering wheel.

"Well, are you going to spill what the hell you mean by 'developments'? Nothing good, I'm sure."

"Your father received several threats."

"Nothing new there." She grunted. "Pricks can't get to him, and it's killing them. He told me all about it."

Oh, if only you knew, Ms. Cross.

That wasn't his problem though. He had a job to do first. And then that was it — no more tours, no more missions, no more contracts. No more. Then he could face what life he had left.

"This is something else. Something new."

The earpiece clicked on once more. "Something's up, looks like. Let me check it."

The channel went dead a moment, then the officer was back on. "Water main break about ten blocks north. Christ."

Lake hated these wrinkles, these little challenges fate and random chance always threw in the way on missions. He didn't like fate or chance — both could get you killed just as dead.

"How long?" He knew the answer before the radio crackled in his ear.

"Hours. Traffic's a mess on the whole upper west side. We'll get you out another route."

"What's going on?" she murmured as the officers flipped on their lights and strobes, their sirens blaring their staccato warning tones as the cruisers picked their way through the slowly moving cars.

"Stay on my ass," the patrolman said in Lake's ear.

"Looks like we're going on a little detour." Lake kept his tone light. "It's nothing."

Her gaze moved from the cruisers, then back to him, the quick movement of her eyes betraying her fear.

It was an absurd time to think it, but he rather liked that look in her eyes.

Not now, Lake. Just get this over with.

As their little convoy snaked through the traffic-snarled streets of New York, he ran over the plan for the next few hours in his mind once again. So much could still go wrong, so much should go wrong — but he knew it wouldn't.

Hit the marks, Lake. Timing. Timing. Timing.

His employer knew what he was doing hiring the company. Lake would perform this last mission, this last task, and he'd do it well — no matter how unpleasant, even wrong, it might be. Right and wrong weren't part of this equation. Only the mission, the job, mattered now.

He'd fulfill his contract, and then he'd be done.

Captive, Mine

For good.

CHAPTER 2

I stared out the window at New York City traffic as our motorcade made its way around the mess.
Every time I'd glance over at Lake, he would meet my gaze so I determined to stop looking at him. I'd just sit quietly. He wouldn't tell me where we were going and I guess that was part of his job. Part of his "keeping me safe." That made me fume.

I could still feel where he'd touched me when he had strapped me in and as much as I wanted to push the button and unlock the seat belt, instinct told me not to do it, not to test him. I wasn't used to being told what to do. Hell, I was the one who did the telling most of the time. Daddy's business, I wasn't a part of that. He made sure to keep me far from it. But I wasn't stupid either. Drug money paid for my apartment, my clothes, my car.

My car...I missed it already. It was a little black BMW M6 Convertible. I tugged at the too tight seat belt, giving him the meanest look I could muster. Screw him. Who was he anyway? A bodyguard. I called the shots, not him.

Captive, Mine

* * *

"How much longer?" I checked my watch. Almost four hours had passed since we'd left the city.

He glanced at me as if only now realizing I was still sitting there.

I raised my eyebrows. "Time? How much longer until we get to where we're going?" I shifted in my seat, trying to get comfortable but failing.

"We'll stop for the night in a few more hours."

"Hours?"

He nodded. He was deep in thought and obviously didn't feel like answering my questions.

"I need to pee," I said, smiling when he glanced at me. I didn't really but he didn't need to know that. Why make this ride pleasant for him when it was anything but for me?

"We just passed a rest stop. You couldn't have mentioned it earlier?"

"You can take this next exit. There's a Starbucks a few blocks off the highway. I could use a cup of coffee too."

"We're not taking another detour." He didn't even bother looking at me when he said it. "We'll stop at the next rest area."

"I have to go *now*," I said, wiggling a little. "You don't want me to have an accident in your truck, do you?" As I said it, I looked in the backseat. It was immaculate; he obviously took care of it. The only thing there was a toolbox on the floor. "I'd feel terrible if I messed up your truck," I added when he met my gaze, my tone as flat as possible.

"Try to be a big girl and hold it, Lily. We're not stopping."

"You're being a jerk."

He said nothing to me, but kept his eyes on the road, passing the exit, mumbling some words into his mouthpiece.

"Where is my new home going to be anyway?"

"I only know the details for tonight's stop. We'll know

more about the final destination tomorrow."

"Okay, then how about tonight? Where are we stopping?"

He turned to me and forced his lips to form a smile. "Holiday Inn."

"Why are you being so mean? I'm the one whose life is over."

He looked at me when I said it and there was one brief moment of emotion in his eyes. Something about that made me take notice, especially when in the next instant, it was gone.

He exhaled. "We'll spend the night near Columbus, Ohio. From there, I really don't know. I won't until tomorrow morning when we head out again. It's another few hours at least to get to our destination. Why don't you close your eyes and get some rest?" he asked, sounding almost nice for a second.

I shook my head and looked forward. I couldn't believe this was happening to me. I had a life, friends. I had everything. I looked out the passenger window to hide the tears that filled my eyes. I was not going to cry. Not in front of him.

At least our escort had lost the marked cars with their blaring sirens. Now three dark sedans followed us while another led the way up ahead.

* * *

"Ms. Cross."

Someone shook my shoulder.

"Wake up, Ms. Cross. We're here."

I opened my eyes and sat up, my body stiff from the awkward position I'd apparently fallen asleep in.

"Get off me." I shrugged off his touch, feeling disoriented and at an even greater disadvantage. I hadn't meant to fall asleep.

He chuckled, opened his door and stepped out. I unbuckled my seatbelt and flipped the visor down, quickly checking my face in the mirror. My hair was tangled where I'd slept on it and my eyes were red. I pushed the visor closed and looked around. We were parked outside a Holiday Inn that looked like it hadn't been renovated since the seventies. The lot was dark and as I watched, Lake picked up a rock and threw it at the lamp closest to the truck, effectively blacking out this part of the parking lot.

"What are you doing?" I asked, climbing out. And I mean climbing. The truck was higher off the ground than I'd expected. He walked over to me as I looked around. "Where are the other cars?" Our motorcade was absent.

When he came close enough that I could see his face, something made me take a step back as a shiver ran through me. A familiar shiver. "Where is everyone?"

One of the sedans came around the corner as I asked the question. I exhaled, feeling, for some reason, relieved. Lake was still watching me when I looked back at him. He smiled but something wasn't right. I could feel it.

"Here they are," he said, stepping to the side and gesturing for me to go ahead of him.

I took a step, taking care not to touch him as I passed between him and the car door. He slammed it shut. One of the officers approached him and handed over a key.

"You have adjoining rooms. 206 and 208, Mr. Freeman," he said to Lake.

"We won't need adjoining rooms," I argued, shivering in the cool night. "Where's my coat?"

The officer opened his mouth to say something but Lake stopped him and turned to me, taking my arms, squeezing once as if he were trying really hard to be patient. "We're here for a few hours to get some sleep. We'll be leaving early tomorrow morning, likely before daybreak. You will take the room you've been assigned and thank the officer for it. You'll also leave the door between our rooms open for the night. Unless of course you prefer I just sleep in your bed."

The officer gave him one look and walked away. I would have slapped him if I hadn't been caught so off guard. "How dare you?" Shaking myself free from his grip, I snatched one of the two keys from his hand before he could stop me. I then straightened up and looked him right in the eye. "*You* work for *me*, Lake Freeman. Remember it."

Rage like a fire brightened his eyes. His mouth tightened into a thin line and he fisted and un-fisted his hands. My heart raced but I somehow managed not to take a step back.

"No, Ms. Cross," he said, taking my wrist and squeezing hard enough that I had to let him have the key. "I work for your father. I do not work for *you*. Remember it."

He twisted my arm upward, keeping hold of my wrist. I tried to yank it away but couldn't.

"You're going to need to check your attitude here and now. You do not want to piss me off."

"What? What are you going to do to me? Everything I have is gone. Nothing you can do can make my situation worse!"

He squeezed so hard I couldn't help but let out a small squeal.

"Mr. Freeman?" the officer said from a few feet away.

Lake glared at me and it took him a moment before he finally let me go. "Move."

I did. I rubbed my wrist which I knew would be

bruised tomorrow, but I moved. I'd met some of Daddy's "associates". They were not a bunch to be fucked with. But in all these years, no one scared me like Lake Freeman scared me now.

The motel was much as I expected: old and gross. Lake let me into my room and told me to stay put. He then took the key and shut the door. I set my bag on the desk and walked over to the window. The curtains had been drawn shut and the window overlooked the highway so I left them as they were. I pulled the covers back from the bed touching as little as possible, wrinkling my face. I didn't stay in hotels like this. This was disgusting.

The bathroom at least looked somewhat clean. The fan went on along with the light. The bright fluorescent light. It didn't do anything for my overall appearance at the moment but at least they did have thick, newer-looking towels. I switched on the shower, letting it steam up the bathroom as I stripped off my dress and underwear, and made sure to lock the door before stepping under the hot stream.

I stayed there for a long time not doing anything at all. The water poured over me and I let myself cry, trying to make as little sound as possible. For the first time in my life, I had no control over what was happening to me. I didn't even know where we were going or what time we'd be leaving.

I did have one thing they didn't know about though: cash and the key to a safe deposit box to access a passport and more funds from a bank in the city were kept in a secret pocket sewn into my purse. No one would know about those things; my dad had arranged it all when I'd moved out on my own once I'd turned eighteen. I'd thought then that he was being overprotective, but now I was grateful that he'd planned so far ahead. That gave me pause to think though. Lake Freeman would not be an easy man to lose. I wondered for a moment why my dad had hired him. It wasn't like him to do something like that without letting me know. Unless he wasn't able to let me know. Could the situation be even more dangerous than I realized?

If I could get back to the city, I could maybe disappear on my own. At least for a while, until Randall was put away for good. I could go to Europe, spend a few years in the South of France.

The thought of my dad all alone somewhere surrounded by much the same as what I was surrounded with here crowded my mind. I knew at once that I couldn't do anything for him. He too had known what was coming but hadn't had much choice in things. Maybe after Randall's trial though. Maybe once it was all over, we could see each other again.

I didn't like what my dad did. I didn't like who he was in this world. Maybe because of his life though, I had stayed clean all of mine. I'd never even smoked a single cigarette. I missed him and as much as I didn't like how he made his money, I also depended on it, knew it provided for everything and then some. I knew the cost, but had always managed to look the other way. Was I as guilty as him for that?

The water began to cool and I switched off the shower.

My father had hired Lake Freeman to protect me, which meant he didn't trust the feds to do it. No big surprise there, I was probably better off dead to them anyway. One less thing to keep my dad from testifying. But Lake was my bigger problem. I didn't trust him; something was off with him. It was just a feeling. I had no concrete evidence of anything. But over the years, I'd learned to trust my intuition. I would try to sneak out tonight when everyone was asleep. Surely they all had to sleep sometime. I'd just have to figure out how to get the keys to Lake's truck.

I squeezed the moisture from my hair and wrapped a towel around myself before opening the bathroom door and stepping into the bedroom, gasping when I did.

"What the hell are you doing?" I asked, holding my towel up with one hand while yanking my purse out of Lake's hands with the other.

He let me have it and remained seated while taking the battery out of my phone. "They should have taken this already. Can't take a chance on anyone tracking you," he said, standing and slipping phone and battery into the back pocket of his jeans. "Good shower?" he asked, looking me over.

"You can't just come in here when you damn well please and you can't go through my purse and take my things!" I looked inside, checking to see if he'd found the secret pocket, but it didn't look like he had. "And give me back my phone. I have my life stored in there."

"You won't be needing it anymore. Remember, you're getting a brand new life now."

I stared at him. He had zero compassion. There wasn't even a hint of emotion in his eyes. I hadn't done anything to deserve what was happening. None of this was my fault. I didn't want this. I hadn't asked for it. And he was treating *me* like a criminal.

I did the only thing I could do. I lunged at him, surprising him long enough to push him onto the bed. "Give me back my things!"

I fell on top of him. One of my hands curled into a fist and, without a thought, I went to punch him. I'd never hit someone before and I'd certainly never punched anyone, but all it took from him was the slightest shift of his body and my fist landed on his shoulder instead of his face. In the next instant, he had me by my wrists and somehow, flipped me over so I lay on the bed on my back pushing against him. But I was no match for his strength. My knee traveled upward but he trapped my leg easily between his thighs and held my arms out on either side of me, his body closer than I liked, his face much closer than I liked.

"Let me go," I spat, trying once more to get free of him but failing. He put more pressure on my wrists until they hurt. "You're hurting me!"

"Then stop fighting and I won't have to!"

"I hate you!" I hissed, feeling my face crumple. "I hate you so much!" I turned away when I started to cry. I hated myself for that.

He shifted his weight and released my wrists. I didn't look at him but rolled over onto my side, tucking my knees up to my chest and hiding my face in my arms.

"Get some sleep," he said, his voice quiet. He switched off the lamp by the bed. I heard the door between our rooms open but didn't hear it close. I stayed as I was, hoping to push every tear that was left out. Hoping to be finished with crying. Knowing I was far from it.

CHAPTER 3

The cold of the early morning bit the exposed skin of his face, his breath fogging before him in the chill air. His mind was elsewhere though, on the woman still inside the motel. Lake checked his watch. 5:10. Still over an hour until dawn. Still enough time to change his mind about this insanity.

But he knew he wouldn't.

The glass doors of the lobby entrance opened haltingly, one of the rollers screeching in its carriage. The hulking form of the state patrol sergeant emerged, his tan Stetson with the purple band perched straight atop his high-and-tight haircut.

"Sleep well, Sergeant?"

The man gave Lake a faint smile utterly devoid of warmth, then sipped from the white lid of his paper coffee cup. "She up yet?"

"Any minute." Lake pointed to the Crown Victoria in the side parking lot, its white exhaust rendering the glare of the headlights into ghostly beams. "She's been briefed on the hand-off. Out the side entrance, 5:15."

"Why the side? Why didn't you bring her out?" The sergeant put a huge fist over his mouth, stifling a cough.

"All that matters is that we got her here. Delivered, safe and sound. But the marshals take things from here." Lake shrugged, feeling the first chill of the air through his heavy coat. "They made it a condition of Cross's deal. Don't really have much leverage to argue with them."

The trooper fixed Lake with a cold stare. "I'd have never let you come this far, if it were up to me."

He gave the trooper a grim smile. "Why did you then?"

"What the DA wants, the DA gets. Like you said — not much leverage to argue with."

Lake looked around. "Where'd your back-up go?"

"Sent 'em home last night." The trooper's flinty gaze looked him up and down. "I've got things handled."

A shadow crossed the beams of the car's lights, the mist of the exhaust swirling. Lily's form paused in front of the vehicle. She was bundled in a dark mid-length coat, the hood lined with ash-colored fur. Her luminous eyes looked back, catching the gleam of the lights.

Lake gave her a nod.

Almost there, bad girl.

The driver's side door opened, a tall, slender man walking around the front, buttoning up his brown jacket. Lily moved back a step, watching the man closely, then glancing back toward Lake. The man said something to Lily, opening his coat and showing her something in his hand. She nodded. The man touched her gently on the upper arm, then ambled over to Lake and the trooper.

"Deputy United States Marshal DeSalvo. WITSEC." The man showed his identification, the distinctive gold star next to the photo and credentials. He gave the trooper a wide, amiable smile, a well-trimmed beard darkening his jawline. "Sergeant Foster?"

"Good to meet you," the trooper said, shaking his hand. He quirked an eyebrow at the marshal. "Just you?"

The marshal cocked a thumb toward his car. "My partner hates the cold. Florida native." He shook his head, rolling his eyes.

The trooper chuckled. "She's all ready for you. No problems getting her out of the city."

"Good. Thank you for all your help, Sergeant." DeSalvo glanced at Lake then back to the trooper, his expression cooling. "This him?"

"Ah yes. Private security for Ms. Cross."

"Lake Freeman." He extended his hand. "I thought you marshal guys had a tin star?"

DeSalvo glanced down at Lake's hand then back to the sergeant. "Only on television, *Mister* Freeman."

The trooper cleared his throat, his square jaw clenching. "I don't like it any more than you do, DeSalvo. DA was very clear though. Freeman goes with her."

The marshal looked down, cursing under his breath. Then he gave the trooper a half smile and shook his hand once more. "Transfer is complete, Sergeant. Thanks again."

"Do you need me to ride along? I can bring you to the state line, at least."

"I'm afraid not, Sergeant." DeSalvo gave a dismissive wave in Lake's direction. "As much as I'd like better company, WITSEC requires we travel without escort."

"Right, I got it. She disappears." Foster tightened the chinstrap on his hat. "Well, it's your show now. Have a good day, Marshal."

The trooper turned away, only giving Lake the smallest of nods. "Freeman."

Prick.

DeSalvo stepped close. "One thing, Mister Freeman. You're tagging along *only*. You do what I say, when I say. Clear?"

Lake snorted, holding out his hand toward the car and the waiting Lily. "Shall we?"

"You wait right here. I'm going to speak with Ms.

Cross first."

DeSalvo walked back to Lily, and they spoke for a moment. The marshal looked back at him, scowling, Lily's voice rising, a finger jabbed in Lake's direction.

The girl had fire, there was no doubt about that. The apple didn't fall far from the tree with the Cross clan. Too bad she used that fire to run that smart mouth of hers. Then the image of her on her knees, looking up at him with fright in her eyes, popped into his mind. Keeping those kind of thoughts away was something he had to do — no exceptions.

He turned away, rubbing a palm over his lips. He wasn't about to fuck up this last job because he couldn't keep his shit wired tight. No, there was no room for this. Not now, not ever. There was only this one last step, then none of it would matter anymore.

It's going to matter a helluva lot to her.

But that couldn't be helped anymore. Perhaps once — but that Lake was gone now. He shook his head, cursing under his breath.

DeSalvo opened the front passenger door, helping Lily inside with a hand on her arm. Then, straightening his jacket, he walked back toward Lake. DeSalvo raised a hand with a smile as the sergeant pulled out of the parking lot with a short, sharp squawk of the cruiser's PA system.

"So"—the marshal glanced back at the idling car with Lily inside—"you ready to do this?"

"Of course. You went a little far with that 'by-the-book' shtick, don't you think?"

"Eh, it's fun, you know? Gotta have fun with this shit when you can." DeSalvo cracked a grin devoid of warmth or compassion, his white canines gleaming in the low light giving him a predatory mien. "You're welcome to sample her before it's done. Boss doesn't care as long as it's done — really done. Quick, clean. No mess."

Lake felt the hair on the back of his neck stand up. "The deal was delivery, that's it."

"And you'll get your cut." DeSalvo tipped his back toward the car. "No sense in passing up a good thing though while you're at it. Perks of the job? She's a little piece. Even better than I thought. Almost a shame, really."

Ransoming the little brat was one thing. He knew how much she meant to Emmanuel Cross, and once he got wind that the cartel had her, Lake knew the man would nix everything. He'd sit in a jail cell until the end of time waiting for his daughter to be returned. Once the case fell apart, the DA would have no choice but to take what he had and throw everything at Cross. She'd be released, but her father would know: as long you're in prison, you continue to keep your mouth shut — because she'll always be there, still vulnerable.

The cartel stays safe, and she stays safe. There was a time Lake would have bristled at the very idea of a job like this, but that time was no longer. The Cross family was of no concern to him — even though he'd been hired by the one to protect the other.

They were accessories to drug dealers. Perhaps she wasn't, *technically* — but she sure wasn't an angel either. It didn't matter anymore though. It was the last run, the final job. And he'd end it there.

One last mission... then he'd be done with what he'd become. And the world would be rid of Lake Freeman and the work he was so good at.

This was something else *entirely*. Brutalizing and defiling a captive was not anything he'd ever sign up for. This was not part of the plan, something outside mission parameters. His mind raced, weighing timing, risks, chances, likelihood of success. Improvisation was rare and dangerous — but it was sometimes a necessary evil. The bitter irony that it would be so urgently called for now on the last mission of his career was not lost on Lake.

DeSalvo was sloppy, but he was dangerous too. Lake had checked out the background of all the cartel goons he could, and DeSalvo, corrupt though he was, still would be

Captive, Mine

a problem.
   A US Marshal-sized problem.

* * *

Lily looked back at Lake from the front seat with a twist of her lips. "Why are you sitting back there?"

"Mr. US Marshal doesn't like me very much."

"A lot better scenery," DeSalvo said softly, looking left as he changed lanes, the engine thrumming pleasingly as he worked the Crown Victoria around a slower-moving eighteen-wheeler.

Lily snapped a look at DeSalvo, her mouth opening, then faced forward once again. She'd kept her coat on, even with the heater working nicely. The eastern sky was just beginning to lighten behind them.

"Where are you taking us, Mr. DeSalvo?"

"Rick, please," he said, giving her a quick smile that looked to Lake like a death totem. "I'll give you the details when we get closer. Protocol, sorry."

She waved a hand, with a small, resigned sigh.

"I've got a question, Ms. Cross." DeSalvo reached into the pocket of his coat, retrieving a pair of leather gloves. He alternated holding the wheel with one hand and then the other, pulling the gloves on with his teeth. "What would you be prepared to do to save your life?"

Lily's big eyes turned slowly to DeSalvo. "I don't... what's that supposed to mean?"

Lake felt his heartbeat pick up speed, thudding in his chest now. He quietly opened the small black case with a snick of the hasp. The cloth was in a clear plastic bag, and he pulled it out, careful to keep it at arm's length.

"I mean, what if you were about to be killed?" DeSalvo rested his elbow on the back of his seat. "Is there *anything* you wouldn't do to survive?"

"You're creeping me the fuck out with—"

Lake lunged forward, clamping his left arm down across her chest, just above the rise of her breasts, pulling back hard. His right hand pressed the cloth to her face, but not hard enough to completely cut off her air. The chemical would do its work as she drew in that first huge, panicky breath, her body readying to fight. She writhed under his grip, her strength surprising, and — shockingly, to him — not exactly unappealing either. Her voice shrieked against the cloth, her hands scratching first at the arms of his coat, then her nails scoring deep furrows of white-hot pain down the back of his hand. In moments, the strength drained from her like water through a sieve, and she finally stilled, her arms dropping into her lap.

It was done, and now there was no going back.

CHAPTER 4

It was cold. I woke up in a pitch-black room lying on something relatively soft, a mattress maybe, on my side, hands bound behind my back and something covering my mouth. I inhaled a deep, shaky breath, telling myself not to panic, which was impossible. I huddled into myself, shivering, trying not to move, mentally scanning my body for injury, which, apart from aches of where I'd been manhandled, I didn't find.

There was no sound in the room aside from my own breathing. I opened my eyes but could see nothing — it was too dark. The last thing I remembered were DeSalvo's words, the look on his face, then being pinned back to the seat, Lake holding me with a cloth pressed against my nose and mouth. Chloroform. He'd held it there until I had passed out.

Something scurried across the mattress and I gasped and tried to scream but the tape over my mouth prevented that. I sat up, my eyes adjusting to the darkness. I was alone. Or at least I thought I was alone. The room had no windows of any kind. The only light that penetrated was that from beneath a door which looked to be that of a garage. I could make out several boxes stacked against the walls but that was all. I wondered if I was in some sort of storage unit.

There was some movement outside then. I tried to stand but that was difficult with my hands cuffed behind my back, so I made noise — as much as I could from behind the tape.

The garage door opened. I squinted against the too-bright fluorescent light blocked only by his form. His large, thick body taking up too much space as he stood, a set of keys dangling from one hand, his clothes slightly disheveled, a smearing of what might have been blood across his shirt.

I sat on my knees and stared up at him, my bodyguard. The grin with which I was met chilled me and I couldn't make another sound. I think my heart stopped altogether for a moment then.

"Cold in here," Lake said, looking around the storage unit.

When he took a step toward me, I sat back on my heels. It was all I could do to put some space between us.

He ignored me completely and rifled through one of the boxes, selecting whatever he was looking for and tucking it into the waistband of his jeans. I thought I glimpsed the black metal of a pistol but he covered it with his shirt too quickly for me to see.

"How long have you been up?"

I tried to ask what the fuck he thought he was doing but it only came out as one jumbled noise from behind the tape covering my mouth.

"What's that?" he asked, reaching for me.

I almost fell over when I tried to back up but he grabbed my arm and hauled me to my feet. The first thing I did was bring my knee up to his crotch. Or attempted to at least.

"Hey!" he said, as if he were issuing some command to a dog. "Play nice." He squeezed my arm hard. "A little gratitude for saving your fucking life would be nice."

I exhaled hard through my nose and stood still, waiting for him to soften his hold on me. When he did, I attacked again, this time managing to connect my knee to his crotch.

He released me and doubled over, but his eyes never left mine. I stood there staring at him for a second before the instinct to run kicked in. But I'd barely taken one step when he gripped the neck of my coat and tugged hard enough that I fell onto the mattress. He was beside me in an instant, pushing me onto my back, his hand around my throat.

"Be good, Lily," he said, reaching into his pocket to take out a Ziploc bag with what I knew to be the chloroform-drenched cloth inside. "I could knock you out until we get to where we're going, but I'm trying to be nice."

I made some noise, wanting the gag off, wanting to know what was going on. I figured he didn't want me dead. He would have killed me already if that were the case. Where was the US Marshal? What was it he'd said last night? *"Is there anything you wouldn't do to survive?"*

Lake was watching me and he seemed to relax as I did. I wanted him to take the gag off. I made some small noise of surrender, a temporary surrender, which he seemed to understand since he smiled.

"You want the tape off?"

I nodded desperately.

"You going to be quiet?"

I nodded again. It was less enthusiastic this time.

"I'm going to stand you up now and we're going to walk to my car. Once there, I'll take it off. If you're good. If not, it stays on for the rest of the drive, understand?"

Yes, I understood. I had zero choice.

"Good girl," he said, standing and hauling me to my

feet.

I imagined there wasn't anyone around if he was going to walk me to his car so obviously against my will so I went along with him. He kept one hand on me as he secured the door of the unit and we walked down the deserted corridor and outside. It was daylight, late afternoon I'd say, and we were alone. In the distance, I could hear the sounds of a freeway but the storage facility itself was in the middle of nowhere.

We walked to a parked black truck similar to the one we'd driven in when we had left the city. The windows on this one however were tinted black. It was the only vehicle in the lot.

He unlocked the passenger-side door and gestured for me to enter. I couldn't help but glance once more at the red stain on the front of his shirt, not at all sure I wanted to know what it was. I stepped a foot up but bound as I was, Lake had to help me in. He closed the door once I was inside and walked over to the driver's side. After climbing in, he made a point of opening the glove compartment and placing what he'd taken from the box into it. He then locked the compartment. I'd been right: it was a revolver.

"Turn your back to me," he said, fishing in his pocket for something.

My eyes grew wider and I shook my head.

He held up the small key. "I'll cuff your hands in front of you. It will be more comfortable," he began, then made a show of putting the key away again. "But if you'd prefer…"

I shook my head no and did as he said, keeping one eye on him over my shoulder. When he unlocked the cuffs, I immediately reached for the tape at my mouth.

"Uh-uh," he said, taking my hand and re-cuffing me, then placing my hands in my lap.

I started to say something about doing what he'd said, that we had a deal, but he just sat back and listened to the jumble of sound until I stopped.

"No screaming, no hysterics when I take it off, understood?"

I nodded and he took a corner of the tape.

"This might hurt a little," he said with a grin on his face as he yanked the tape off.

"Ow! Fuck you!" My hands covered the area around my mouth. That was worse than the worst waxing session I'd ever had!

He ignored me and reached to strap me in, nice and tight like the first time he'd done it. I didn't miss his glance at my chest and when he met my gaze again, I made sure he knew I knew.

"My dad's going to kill you," I said, my voice low.

He started the truck. "Your dad's going to thank me. That and pay me a nice bonus."

"You're as good as dead, Lake Freeman."

"I don't think so," he said, merging onto the highway.

"Where are you taking me? What happened to the US Marshal?" I looked out the window but didn't recognize anything. "Where are we?" It was strange how I heard the tone of my own voice changing with that last question. I glanced back over at him, really looking at him. He was big with thick, muscular arms and legs. Under any other circumstances, I might have found him attractive, but not today. Today I was scared. Something had gone wrong in the plan to whisk me away to a new life. It wasn't that I felt broken up over that. I didn't want to leave my old life behind. But the fact that I was here, handcuffed, in a car with Lake Freeman, alone, meant my father's enemies had gotten to him. It didn't make sense though. Where was DeSalvo? My gaze returned to that spot on Lake's shirt just as he looked at me.

"Where we are and where you're going don't matter. What does matter is that if I'd gone through with the original plan, you'd be Randall's guest right now and the only bargaining chip they have to buy your father's silence.

DeSalvo was in on it."

He caught me glancing once more at that stain but didn't elaborate, nor did I want him to.

"What about you then? You were in on it too?"

He only nodded once, his face suddenly, incredibly hard.

"I don't understand." I brought my bound hands to my face and rubbed.

He glanced at me and exhaled, shaking his head and for one moment, emotion flashed across his eyes. It was gone as quickly as it had come however, and he grinned. "I figured I could make more money selling you back to Daddy."

The way he said that last part was a taunt but I refused to take the bait. There was more to his story. My dad would have paid him a hefty sum to protect me, and double-crossing Randall meant a death sentence.

I shook my head, thinking this through. It didn't make sense. "You're leaving something out, *Lake*. My dad would have paid you well to protect me. Randall would have topped that for delivering me to him. Doesn't make sense that you'd double cross both of them. What are you not telling me?"

His jaw tightened and I knew I was right. He didn't speak for a while. In fact, it was a good while before he said another word. Instead, he put on his blinker and crossed multiple lanes to get off at the next rest area. When he did park the truck and finally, slowly, turned to me, I shuddered at his expression. He leaned a little closer, making every hair on my body stand on end.

"Maybe I just like to keep pretty girls chained to my bed."

I could only stare at him. I didn't breathe, my mouth didn't open, I didn't have words or thoughts or anything at all. Every inch of me vibrated with sudden, primal fear. My instinct wasn't to fight, it was to run. I think if he'd stayed as close as he had been for even another second, I would have screamed. Or worse, broken down in tears. But he didn't. Instead, he took the key out of the ignition.

"Do you need to use the restroom?" he asked.

"Yes," I said, my voice weaker.

He took that time to open the glove compartment and retrieved the small revolver. "Do you think you can be a good girl and do as I say when we're inside or do you think I should drive to a more secluded area where you can piss along the side of the road while I watch?"

"I'll be good," I said quickly, my eyes on the gun.

"What will happen if you're not?" he asked.

My chest felt tight at his words.

"Cat got your tongue?" he asked.

"You'll hurt me," I answered, looking directly at him.

"I'm glad we understand each other. Hold out your hands."

I did so without hesitation and watched while he unlocked the cuffs. I rubbed my wrists, my brain already working out a plan. Any plan. The way I saw it, my options were very limited. My best chance at escape was when we were in public, when there were people around. I wondered then if anyone was even looking for me. If anyone knew the original plan had gone wrong, so terribly wrong, but I doubted it. It wasn't as if the feds were looking out for my best interests. They were doing what they needed to do to get my dad to testify.

"Let's go," he said, climbing out of the truck.

He came around to my side and opened the door, took my arm and "helped" me out. He then locked the truck and wrapped his big hand around mine, squeezing hard enough to make me wince. He looked down at me and smiled as we passed a family with small children. We then entered the building, which contained a small convenience store and restrooms. There were maybe a dozen people inside and two cashiers. He walked me not to the ladies room but to the large and private handicap bathroom. It was when we went inside it together that I dug my heels in.

"I am not going to go to the bathroom in front of you!"

He ignored me and unzipped his pants.

"What are you doing?" I asked, backing up when he let me go.

"I'm taking a leak," he said. "If it so offends you, then don't watch."

My mouth opened and closed but when he proceeded to take himself out of his jeans, I quickly looked away, not missing his chuckle.

"I can't believe you're doing this!"

He didn't respond. Instead, he flushed the toilet when he was finished.

He washed his hands and plucked two paper towels out of the dispenser to dry them. "Your turn," he said, standing back as if to watch.

"I don't think so. You can wait outside."

He shrugged a shoulder. "I'll be right on the other side of the door and you will not lock it, understand?"

"Fine."

"Don't try anything," he said before he walked out.

I gave him a smirk and locked the door as soon as he was gone. Jerk.

At least the toilet was clean. Once I was finished, I quickly washed my hands but left the water running.

"You done?" Lake asked from the other side of the door.

"Almost," I said, looking around.

I reached for a paper towel and saw the small cabinet beneath the sink. The lock was loose so I yanked hard and managed to get the door open. Inside were cleaning supplies: an empty bottle of bleach, rags, toilet cleaner, and Windex.

He knocked again. I ignored him and picked up the Windex. I would have preferred the bleach, but this would have to do.

"Open the door, Lily."

"Just a minute," I said, spraying the Windex into the air. If I got him in the face, in the eyes, well, that would hurt and possibly give me the moment I'd need to get help.

I smiled and unlocked the door, and just as I knew he would, he didn't wait for me to open it. Instead, he pushed the door open and stepped inside, already muttering something I couldn't quite make out because once he was in, he pushed the door closed and I extended my arm, aimed for his face, and squeezed.

"Ah! Fuck!" he called out, squeezing his eyes shut with one hand and trying to reach for me with the other.

I squeezed again and almost made it out. I would have made it if it hadn't been for the woman who had reached to open the door in the meantime, her daughter's wheelchair in front of her blocking my exit.

"What's going on in here?" she began.

"Just a minute!" Lake said, taking the opportunity to push the door closed and grab hold of me. He stared at me, furious, while turning on the tap. He kept his hand locked on my arm as he splashed water over his face, his eyes.

"I'm sorry!" I began, stunned at my failed plan. I'd been so close.

The woman knocked again. "This is a handicap restroom!"

Lake made some noise as he towel dried his face. Taking me by the collar of my coat, he pulled me to him. "You are in so much fucking trouble. Keep your mouth shut," he said, making a point of showing me the gun tucked inside the waistband of his jeans.

I shook my head, "I'm so sorry…" I began, but he cut me off.

"No, not yet you're not, but you will be."

* * *

It was very, very close. He'd been sloppy — and there wasn't room for that anymore.

"You're going to walk with me back out to the truck." He stood close enough that his whisper was loud and clear, her wide liquid eyes fixed upon him, her face ashen. "You're going to do *exactly* that, and nothing more. You don't talk — not a single word. You don't resist, you don't run. Got me, Ms. Cross?"

For a moment she simply stared, her mouth open. Then she swallowed, nodding.

"Good."

His hand engulfed hers, squeezing tightly enough that she winced. He liked that. She'd be getting a lot more where that came from in a few minutes.

Striding back across the patched asphalt parking lot, Lily in tow, he scanned the area, going over the possibilities in his mind. None of them were good. But first, he needed to get them moving again. Movement, was life.

Fortunately, the place was practically deserted. But the woman with the girl in the wheelchair might be a problem. He'd glanced back at her as they'd rushed out of the bathroom. The woman's beady eyes, peering over flushed jowls, had watched them the entire time.

Much too closely.

He hoisted Lily up into the back seat of the truck, her body jerking at the loud clatter of a Jake brake sounding from a tractor-trailer racing past on the freeway beyond them.

"Don't move an inch," he rumbled, buckling the belt tight. He cuffed her hands once more, and, fortunately for her, she seemed to be learning, offering her wrists without so much as a peep. He looked behind him once more, just to be sure, then reached for her, a hand tight in the curls of her dark hair.

"No, wait—" she yelped as he slapped the tape over her mouth once more, smoothing it over her soft lips.

His fingers shook as he walked around to the driver's side, his eyes checking the parking lot one last time. With any luck, Lake and Lily would fade out of memory for everyone there, even Ms. Beady Eyes. But it had nearly been disaster.

As he pulled the truck down the on-ramp and accelerated back onto the freeway, he gripped the steering wheel hard, his hands creaking.

Not now, Lake. You can't do it now. You're too pissed.

He breathed slowly, deeply, glancing at her in the rearview mirror. Her eyes met his in the reflection, and what he saw in them made him smile.

Fear.

It was what he wanted to see because if she feared him, maybe she'd listen to him. And if she listened to him, it *might* keep them alive. Simply fearing him wasn't enough though. Not for him.

It was time to teach her to obey him, too.

Watching the road once more, he brought the truck up to just under seventy. Willing himself to calm, he visualized what needed to be done next. There was so little time, and yet being careful, calm was so important. Swiftness, precision, decisiveness. He'd need all of them to get them to safety. And he'd need a little luck too.

Once the scenery turned from suburban to rural, he took an exit that looked suitably deserted, driving away from the freeway until he found a turnabout spot partially screened by a dense stand of tall evergreens. The gravel was loud under his tires as the truck bounced over the edge of the shoulder. It was far enough off the road to be relatively secluded, but not so far as to raise suspicion. He parked and got out, laying both hands on the hot hood and inhaling deeply, the air smelling faintly of the cedars soaring above them.

It was time she learned that first lesson.

Opening the rear passenger door on the driver's side, he climbed in, closing it behind him, the air inside still, quiet. Her chest heaved with her panicky breathing, her nostrils flaring. Her body leaned against her door, as far from him as she could get.

"When I tell you to do something, Ms. Cross, you'd damn well better do it." He brought his face closer to hers, inhaling the clean scent of her perfume. He spoke slowly, steel in his voice.

"You're going to learn to start obeying me. And you want to know why? Because it's going to keep us alive, but more importantly, you'll do it because I told you to. Do you understand?"

Her eyes grew wide, and she looked down at the tape. He reached for it, curling fingers under one corner. "I'll pull this back, and I'd better hear the words: 'Yes, Sir'" His fingers yanked it to the side, leaving it to hang from her flushed cheek

"Fuck, that hurts!" She reached up with her cuffed hands, running fingertips along her lips.

"Those weren't the words I wanted to hear." He batted her hands away, stilling her with a fist twisting in her hair and a slap of the tape back over swollen, reddened lips. "That's going to cost you."

Her eyes narrowed, and enraged, but unintelligible, squalling erupted from behind the tape, two utterances sounding suspiciously close to "asshole."

Not a quick learner, this one.

He found he rather appreciated that — but first it was time to get the beautiful woman's attention. Sliding toward the middle of the rear bench seat, he deftly unlatched her belt. She moved instantly, trying to lunge forward. He threaded his fingers into the rich, silky weight of her hair then clenched his fist. She froze, her eyes squeezing shut with a pained grunt.

Yanking roughly, he pulled her down, drawing her over his lap. Her cuffed hands pushed at his lap as she tried to rise, but he grasped them by the chain linking her wrists, and hauled her hands out in front of her. He yanked her blouse from the clutch of her dark jeans, rucking it up to expose the satin paleness of her lower back.

She kicked out, hard, her heel connecting against the door with a loud thud, and she pushed against it with surprising strength. He twisted his fist in her hair further, and she squealed once more. Pulling one leg from beneath her struggling body, he laid it over the back of her kicking legs, clamping down on them until only her feet drummed against the door. He leaned over her, his lips at her ear.

"You'll lie still, or it'll be worse for you. Nobody knows you're out here. *Nobody*. Be good, and this'll be quick."

Though he wanted this lesson to get through to her, part of him hoped very much that she'd defy his order.

Of course, she struggled and squirmed, no matter how fruitless it was. He allowed himself a grim smile at her fire, knowing it was going to make things all the harder — but knowing it made things all the more interesting too.

The jeans she wore hugged her figure well, and up close, he got the first good glimpse at it. Despite her petite build, her ass was actually quite generous, plump and round, the jeans displaying its curves enticingly.

Survival first, Lake. Then you can indulge yourself.

But that wasn't quite true. She needed to learn — and the faster, the better — that doing what she was told was vital for her, for her very survival — and it was vital for the comfort of that little bubble butt she'd been hiding too.

He'd teach her a lesson, but there was nothing wrong with enjoying himself while he did it.

Pushing her head down steadily, he held her by the hair at the base of her skull, not allowing her an inch of movement. He brought his hand down on her jeans-clad ass once, then again, harder. The rough fabric stung his palm.

She froze, a puzzled little sound coming from behind the tape. Then, as if a switch had been turned on, her entire body writhed in every direction, her hips rising and falling as she struggled against the iron grip of his legs. He felt his cock stir as she moved against him, the feeling of overpowering her with his strength speaking to something deep inside himself he hadn't known was there.

Kidnapping her wasn't enough? Are you planning on adding rapist to your rap sheet too?

He didn't even answer such a ridiculous question, didn't need to. All he intended to do was teach this spirited little woman what happened when she defied him. His fingers insinuated under the waistband of her jeans, the smooth, soft flesh against the back of his hand. He hauled on them, trying to pull them off, but they hugged her hips too tightly. She screeched again, struggling even harder.

"Oh no. I'm not going to fuck you, Lily. Not yet." He reached around her hip, fingers searching for the button in front, undoing it. "But your jeans are giving you way too much protection."

A lost whimper escaped the tape as he worked the jeans roughly down, exposing more of her pale flesh to his gaze. Then he saw the little dark swatch of fabric between her buttocks and laughed.

"A thong? You little slut, Lily." The black lace had worked partially off as he'd pulled down her jeans some more. He yanked the jeans fully clear of her ass, letting them bunch where his thigh clamped down on her legs. His fingers snatched up the lace, and he ripped it down her thighs too, leaving it in a tangled bundle with her jeans.

Her bottom was even more beautiful than he'd imagined: soft, smooth, but its contours surprisingly broad and lush for so slight a frame. Between the tense, trembling thighs, the dark slot below her buttocks invited, hinting at the hidden sex, calling to him despite how wrong this all was.

Get it done, Lake.

"I'd never have guessed you were hiding an ass like this. Little thing like you?" His hand smoothed over the curve of one hip, and she grew very still at the touch of his hand to her warm, bare skin. "That's better. Lie quiet now, and we'll get this over with, Lily."

He palmed the soft curve of her buttock, enjoying the feel of her for just a moment. His cock was fully at attention now, and he tried to ignore it — there'd be time to think about what to do about that later.

Then he began.

He slapped her bottom slowly at first, getting a feel for how hard he needed to smack. Each spank rang out crisply in the confines of the quiet cab, her body vibrating with each blow. He watched the way her white bottom jiggled at each slap, the rich flesh wobbling as he smacked one cheek then the other. He covered each cheek thoroughly with slaps until the flesh glowed a uniform red. His palm rested over the fleshiest part of her bottom.

"What do you think we're up to here, Lily? Do you understand how much danger we're in?"

She snarled unintelligibly behind the tape, arching up, her feet kicking the door.

He spanked her faster then, landing hard smacks in a methodical fashion, making sure the whole of one cheek burned, the color deepening to scarlet, then marching another flurry of smacks up and down the other cheek. He traced a finger along two raised welts left by his blows. Her thighs trembled under his leg, her cries growing more plaintive.

"The first thing you need to learn is to *listen*." He landed a harsh blow where her plump buttock met sleek thigh, the flesh bounding, the scream muffled by the tape. "When I tell you to do something, you *do* it. You don't argue with me. Ever."

His palm cracked down on the same spot three times in quick succession on the lower part of her far bottom cheek, the flesh blazing under his hand, wrenching more cries from her.

"You're not Daddy's little girl out here. You're lost at sea. And I'm your only hope of making it home, Lily." He landed two smacks to the tender flesh of each thigh, and she reared up, shrieking again. "Get it through your head, Ms. Cross. I'm all you've got, and if you don't start acting like it, you're going to be spending a lot of time with a very sore ass."

Truthfully, he was going comparatively easy on her, but she didn't need to know that. Once he got her to their destination, he'd be able to deal with her more effectively, more strictly — how he really wanted to go about demonstrating her new role in life. As pleasing as this little spanking was, she had a lot more — and worse — to look forward to once he finally got them to safety.

There, she'd finally understand she'd been dropped into the deep end of the pool.

He tightened his grip on her hair, pausing to stroke her bottom, the heat radiating from her skin like a furnace. He laid the comparatively cool back of his hand across her inflamed buttocks, and she tensed, whimpering. The feel of her flesh made his cock throb, the hard bulge pressing to her naked hip. He knew he shouldn't let her know this was turning him on — he wasn't quite sure what that meant anyway — but getting her through this, getting this message across was more important.

Landing loud blows across those burning, clenching cheeks, he varied the timing, smacking her once, then waiting, only to land a flurry of hard blows when she least expected it. Concentrating most of the spanks on a narrow band at the base of her buttocks and the tops of her thighs, he kept at her until her keening was continuous, her bottom a deep, swollen crimson, a crazy patchwork of darker welts and handprints over the flushed canvas of her plump buttocks.

Stroking her scorched cheeks, he loosened his grip on her hair. "Now, your punishment is done, as long as you start doing what you're told. Do you think you can do that?"

She dropped her head as far as his grip allowed, her

back hitching.

"I'm not doing this because I want to, Lily."

I'm sure the fact your cock is hard as a rock against her hip doesn't make that a lie right?

"I'm doing this because you need this. You need to learn the truth of things. And I'm going to show it to you." He eased her thong back up, slower than he needed to, enjoying the view a little longer. He seated the black lace tightly between the blazing, enticing bottom cheeks, then pulled her jeans back up, leaving them unbuttoned. He brought her upright, moving her to the sit next to him, her flushed face downcast, eyes brimming tears, dark curls plastered to her forehead.

"Look at me, Lily."

The coffee-brown eyes locked with his, their liquid depths making his heart twist. He saw hurt there, of course, but he saw something else, something that cut deeper than he'd ever expected.

Hatred.

Why the fuck does it matter, Lake?

It didn't — not right now, anyway. The only thing that mattered was that she understood.

"I'm going to take this tape off and wipe your face." Tears, snot, and runnels of dark mascara had made a mess of her much-too-potent beauty. "I'm not going to hear a peep out of you am I? One word, and it's back over my lap. Got it?"

She nodded quickly, more tears welling from those pretty eyes. He didn't want to think about the fact that her tears somehow aroused him even more. What the hell was it with this woman?

Maybe you're just a sadistic fuck.

There didn't really have to be an explanation for it. Maybe it didn't matter anymore.

His thumb stroked through a crazy smear of mascara down her cheek. "It's all done, Lily. As long as you behave."

Fingers pulled the tape away as gently as he could, though she still winced, her eyes closing tightly. She worked her mouth as he balled the tape up in his hand. He reached forward, flipping open the center console storage area and retrieving one of the red shop rags he kept there, thankful he had a couple that were still clean.

He wiped the mess from her face, her cheeks flushed scarlet, her gaze sliding away from his.

"Now, I've still got a ton of driving to do. I need to know you're going to behave yourself back here while I do it." He threw the used rag up onto the front passenger seat then scrubbed his chin with a hand. "Can I trust you to stay quiet? Stay where you are? I might be able to release those cuffs if you can prove you've earned it."

"I won't — I won't do anything. Just don't hurt me."

Lake felt a flare of anger and a little twinge of guilt.

"I'm not here to hurt you, Lily."

All evidence to the contrary.

He looked out the side window at the hunter-green boughs of the cedars swaying in the wind. Then he grunted, shaking his head. "Believe it or not, I'm here to keep you in the drug dealer's daughter business."

"What's that supposed to mean?" Her voice dropped, and she drew a shaky breath. "I mean, I don't get what this is. Why — why are you doing this?"

Lake opened the door and slid out, turning in the doorway to face her. "What is this? This is us trying to stay alive, Lily. We've got a shit-ton of hurt looking for us now, and we need to get to safety so I can figure out what to do next."

He ran a hand roughly through his hair, his palm noticeably sore from spanking Lily's luscious little ass.

"Now, for *why* I'm doing this? I haven't a fucking clue."

CHAPTER 5

I buttoned up my jeans as quickly as I could and looked out the window as Lake drove back onto the highway. The car was quiet; I was quiet. I had nothing to say, I had to process what the hell had just happened, what he'd done to me. I glanced at him, at the side of his head, but when his eyes met mine in the rearview mirror, I quickly dropped my gaze to my lap where my hands rested, still linked together. My nail polish was peeling. With my thumbnail, I scratched it off completely from my fingers, all the while thinking, trying to understand.

He had spanked me. He had taken me over his knee, pulled down my jeans and panties and spanked me. It felt strange, *I* felt strange. I tried to make myself smaller, make myself disappear. When I inhaled, my breath hitched and I could feel his gaze on me again in the mirror. I wasn't going to cry. If he was expecting me to cry then he was going to be disappointed.

The afternoon sun had disappeared now and it was full

night. The window felt cold against my head but I laid it there, watching cars drive by, trying to keep track of the exits we passed but unable to after a while.

Had my father really hired Lake Freeman to guard me or had that been a lie? How had he known our safe word though? Nobody knew that. Hell, I barely remembered it. That was why I had gone so willingly with him. Although I hadn't trusted him, I trusted my dad and if Lake knew those words, then I figured my dad had told them to him.

"Is my dad okay?" I asked, suddenly fearing the worst, wondering if something had happened to my father. Wondering if he'd been forced to give up those words. But why? What would be the point of that?

Lake looked back at me, his expression confused. "I would assume so. Why?"

I shook my head. "Nothing. Never mind."

He turned back to the road, seemingly deep in thought himself. So my father had hired Lake but Lake had been paid by the cartel to kidnap me and deliver me to them. He and DeSalvo both. I didn't want to ask what had happened to DeSalvo. I didn't give a fuck about him. I remembered those last moments in the car before losing consciousness and between DeSalvo and Lake Freeman, I'd have chosen Lake as the safer option.

Lake who just bared your ass and spanked you.

My face felt hot as embarrassment washed over me at the very vivid memory. At least my butt didn't hurt as much anymore. It hurt while he was spanking but the pain had passed quickly. If I could have though, I would rather have kept the physical pain and lost the humiliation of it.

Back to the why. Why not just hand me over to the cartel? He'd have gotten paid. Randall would have kept me alive if only to make sure my father didn't testify against them, but that didn't mean they'd have kept me safe. Hell, they probably would have done a lot worse than spank me by now.

I glanced at the back of Lake's head again. *Asshole.* He

was only the lesser of two evils; it would be good to remember that. And besides, what now? Why save me from the cartel? What was in it for him and what was in store for me?

Maybe I just like to keep pretty girls chained to my bed.

I swallowed, feeling flushed again, only it was different this time.

"I don't understand why you're doing this. They'll kill you when they find you and they *will* find you. They're not going to give up. You're one man against a whole organization. An organization that doesn't exactly put much value on human life — even less if that human life stole from them."

He met my eyes in the mirror. His face was tight and I knew I wasn't telling him anything he didn't already know.

"Remember your promise to be quiet?" he asked.

I narrowed my eyes but when he held up the roll of duct tape, I exhaled and leaned my head back against the window.

* * *

I woke when the truck bounced over a pothole. Shit. Like the last time, I'd fallen asleep. I needed to know where he was taking me. I needed to stay alert.

"Where are we?" I asked, rubbing the heels of my palms over tired eyes.

He maneuvered around the curve and kept driving. We were in the woods somewhere. All I could see were trees, not a single car or house. The road looked to be unpaved and the next potholes sent me bouncing in my seat. A few more minutes of this and in the headlights, I could make out a house.

"Home," he said finally, coming to a stop around the back of the house.

I was suddenly wide awake, looking out both windows for any sign that would tell me where we were.

"Where is this? How long have we been driving?" I cursed myself for not wearing a watch but I'd always used my cell phone to tell the time. I could have been out for hours; I had no idea.

Lake killed the engine, retrieved the pistol from the glove compartment and shoved it into the waistband of his jeans before picking up the tape and climbing out of the truck. He came to my side to open the door.

"We're home, princess. Let's go."

I looked from him to the house and back.

"Need help?" he asked, his eyes hard again, his tone impatient.

I reached over and pushed the button to release my seatbelt. When he held out a hand to help me, I pulled away, climbing clumsily out on my own. He didn't say anything but slammed the door shut then locked the truck. It was cold, colder here than it had been in the city.

"I want my coat." I'd forgotten it in the truck.

"We'll be inside in a minute."

I stood by the truck when he moved toward the house, not sure what I was going to do, not sure of anything at all.

Should I run? Where to? It was pitch black, I had no idea where I was and my hands were cuffed together. But I wasn't going to go willingly into the house.

"Lily," he said, gesturing to the door.

I stared back at him. I couldn't make my legs move if I tried.

"Christ," he said. He walked toward me and took me by the arm, but he had to drag me every step of the way.

"I don't want to go inside." I tried to pull free even though I knew if I did, even if he let me run, there was nowhere to go.

"You'd rather stand out here and freeze?"

"Let me go."

"Once you're inside."

I shook my head. I was scared, that was all there was to it. I was scared.

Maybe he knew I couldn't do what he said even if I wanted to because without a word, he simply turned to the door and dragged me right along with him, releasing me only once we were in the house. He locked the door and switched on one lamp, then walked around to the other side of the couch and switched on another. The cabin wasn't large and furnishings were sparse. It was so cold inside that I would have hugged my arms around myself except for the fact that my hands were still linked to one another.

Lake adjusted the thermostat. He then began stacking wood into the large stone fireplace. The living room contained one sofa and a large, very worn-looking wingback chair. It matched the leather of the couch but for the fact that it was obviously the more used of the two pieces. The coffee table was unremarkable, the dining table square and seated four on stiff, wooden chairs.

"Built the cabin myself," Lake said.

He sat on the natural stone hearth tearing off bits of newspaper for kindling.

I grinned. "Like I give a fuck. You promised you'd take

the cuffs off. I've done as you've said, I've hardly spoken and I've been a *good girl*. Take them off." I held my arms out to him.

He raised his eyebrows then returned his attention to the fire. "Well, your friendly tone of voice certainly encourages me to *do as I'm told.*"

"You promised."

He lit the newspaper and chips of wood and we both watched as the fire grew and the wood began to crackle. He then stood and came toward me. I leaned away from him, his height, his whole person seeming much larger in the cabin.

"Take them off," I repeated, my voice trembling a little now that he stood so close.

"Why don't I show you to your room. You'll be allowed out when you're feeling friendlier."

He took me by the arm and began to walk me toward the corridor.

"Get off me!" I yanked myself free. "Don't fucking touch me. I'm not exactly here of my own free will. You've kidnapped me and you've…" I faltered for a moment and he moved another step toward me. This time, I took two back.

"I've what? Spanked you?" he asked, his expression one that screamed enjoyment.

I gritted my teeth, forcing myself to keep my eyes on his. "What are you going to do to me?" I asked because really, that was the only thing that mattered, right? My entire body prickled at the question and he lost the grin, his face softening a little. But that was momentary.

"That depends on you." He crooked his finger at me, walking over to one of the far windows.

I remained where I was, watching him.

"Come here, Lily," he said when I didn't follow.

I went.

"Out there," he said, pointing to what appeared to be a second structure similar to this one but much smaller.

"I've got a special room out there," he paused, and I could feel his eyes on me while I kept my gaze on the structure. "A room for bad girls."

I looked at him then. The way he said it, drawing out the words *bad girls* most definitely sent a message.

"And I've got another room back here." This time he took my arm and walked me not too gently down the small hallway. "Two, actually. One for me." He opened the first door we came to so I could peek inside. From what I could see, he'd taken special care furnishing that room. "And another for good girls," he said, taking me to the next room and opening the door. This room was half the size of the other and contained one double bed, a nightstand with a lamp on it, and a dresser. "Now, are you going to be a good girl or a bad girl tonight?"

I met his gaze and told him where he could go. At least mentally I did. I wasn't stupid. Not completely. "I'll be good," I said, forcing a neutral tone, vowing vengeance.

"I'm glad to hear it." His face broke into a smile. "Let's get something to eat and we can get some sleep."

"What time is it?"

He checked his watch. "Late." He looked at me, daring me to push him. I would let this one go.

We went back to the dining room where he pulled out one of the chairs and retrieved the key to the handcuffs.

"Sit," he ordered.

I looked at that key and I sat, holding out my hands. He unlocked the cuffs, removed the one from my left wrist and connected my right wrist to the chair.

"Come on! I'm not going anywhere. Where would I go? We're in the middle of some…forest, it's night and you've locked the door!"

"Christ Lily, can't you just sit down and shut the fuck up for five minutes?" he asked.

"Screw you! You sit down. Newsflash, Lake: *you* kidnapped *me*! You'll forgive me if I find it difficult to 'just sit down and shut the fuck up'."

Captive, Mine

I could almost see him counting to ten while I waited, unable to breathe in those few moments. "I've had a long day, Lily," he began unlocking the handcuffs and pulling me to my feet. "And before I do something we both regret, we're going to call it a night."

I had no choice but to follow, regretting my outburst, afraid for his sudden, quiet anger as he all but dragged me down the hall and opened the door to the bathroom.

"I'll ask you exactly once if you need to use the restroom. If you say no, you will not have another opportunity until the morning."

My heart beat so hard against my chest I was sure he could hear it as clearly as I. I nodded fast and he let me go into the bathroom, but when the toe of his boot kept me from closing the door all the way, I stopped.

His arms were folded across his chest and he stood watching me. "Door stays open."

I opened my mouth to protest but closed it again. As fast as I could, I pulled my jeans and panties down and went, not once looking up at him even after I'd flushed and washed my hands. I caught a glimpse of my reflection in the mirror along with his, which loomed behind me. I looked like I felt: scared.

"I'm done," I said, drying my hands on my jeans when I didn't see a hand towel.

He nodded and gestured toward the second bedroom. His earlier words came back to me again: *Maybe I just like to keep pretty girls chained to my bed.* They made me glance over my shoulder at him as we entered the room, he stood so close behind me I swore I could feel his breath at my neck. I wanted to tell him I was sorry. I wanted to go back those ten minutes and sit down and shut up. I had questions only he had the answers to but I had screwed up my chance to ask them and instead pissed him off.

Once inside the bedroom, he pulled the covers back and made me sit on the bed.

"Lie down and give me your hands."

He could do anything he wanted to do to me. I knew it and so did he.

"Lake?" I began, but he cut me off.

"Lie. Down."

"Please don't hurt me. I'm sorry. I'm just—"

"Lie the fuck down!" he snapped.

I think I was down before he finished the sentence. He didn't ask me to give him my hands this time. Instead, he took them and cuffed me to the iron railings that made up the headboard. At least I was too scared to cry. I only watched as he pulled my boots from my feet and set them on the floor before drawing the blankets up to my shoulders and standing back to have one more look at me before walking out the door.

It was only after he was gone that I began to cry.

CHAPTER 6

As he stared at the flickering, dancing flames, he wondered what was wrong with him.

The room was as dark as night, only the orange light of the fire to keep him company. There were probably dozens of trained killers already on the road, looking for him, ready to claim what Randall saw as his. But rather than think about that, about what had to be done, he could only think of one thing.

The woman lying alone in her room, twenty-five feet away.

"You're in some shit here, Lake. How the hell are you getting out of this?"

He'd thought getting to the cabin would calm his nerves, would give him a base to prepare, to formulate a plan to survive the next seventy-two hours. But rather than calm him, his nerves were as keyed up as they'd ever been. She was still here, and now that the flight was over — for now, anyway — that was what he kept coming back to. He couldn't ignore the door that had been opened when he'd spanked her, the thrill he'd felt with her under his control, at the thought of what he'd do once he'd gotten her here.

There was no putting that genie back in the bottle.

The fire popped, the faint orange of a cinder fading on the black stone of the hearth. He propped an elbow on the arm of the chair, resting his chin on his hand. He needed to sleep, especially now, while they had time. He figured there was better than an even chance they'd left no trail, but he needed to plan for what happened if his calculation was off, for what happened when they came for them.

Came for her.

The crazy mix of possessiveness and protectiveness he felt surge through him at that thought shook him, surprising him with the power of it.

"No time to get attached, Lake," he murmured against the heel of his hand. "You know what needs to be done about that, don't you?"

He checked the locks at the front and back doors, cursing as he dashed his hip against the counter in the dark kitchen. He stood outside her room, asking himself the question once more, silently cursing the fact he didn't have a plan for this, for the vexing young lady currently in his custody.

He left her door closed.

As he curled up on the couch, a blanket retrieved from the closet wrapped around him, two possible paths became clear — one that filled him with dark anticipation, and one that he knew was right.

Before he could decide which to follow, he slipped off to sleep.

* * *

A faint light had begun to bleed into the room, the dawn still an hour or so away. He leaned against the doorway, arms crossed against the morning chill. She'd kicked the blanket down to her waist in the night, and he could see the sheen of sweat at the hollow of her throat. Letting her sleep in her clothes wasn't the best idea he'd ever had.

Her blouse had bunched underneath her, pulling up in front, baring her belly, the dark well of her umbilicus. Her hair was a wild spray of black curls, a lock of it lying across her cheek. He stepped to the bed, taking a moment to look down the length of her lithe body, then inserting the key into each cuff. He pulled her wrists free, the cuffs clanging against the wrought iron of the headboard posts. He knew her shoulders were probably sore from being bound this way, but he needed to be sure she didn't try anything while he slept. She was smart and resourceful, along with being stubborn and disobedient.

He brushed the lock of hair from her cheek, feeling the silky curl between his fingertips. Her lips were parted, allowing a glimpse of those perfect white teeth. For a moment, he just stood there, listening to her breathe, feeling again how much he missed that quiet, soft sound. One of the million things he'd lost when he'd lost his wife, when he'd lost the last reason to do what was right.

Lily turned away, the soft pink of her lips moving in an unintelligible murmur, her legs curling up as she tucked her newly freed arms in front of her. The position emphasized the flare of her hips in those tight jeans, the shape of that heart-shaped ass already making his cock stir once more.

Down, boy.

He needed to check her. He trusted her father even less than he trusted Randall. It might already be too late. The idea of doing it while she still slept should have been less appealing than it really was, but instead he had another idea. Another lesson that could be taught.

He patted the curve of her jeans-clad bottom.

"Time to get up, Lily. Got a long day ahead of us."

The growl she made was half-irritated and half-plaintive.

"Come on, let's go." He took hold of her hip, shaking her. "Up."

Her groan made him smile, biting his lip to submerge it.

"My arms are ... killing me." She rolled back over, facing him, eyes half open, her hands squeezing the muscles of her upper arms. "Why'd you cuff me?"

"Can't have you wandering off, can we?" Lake kicked a boot against the side of the mattress. "Get out of bed. You're getting a shower — but there's something we take care of first."

"Shower?" Her voice perked, and her eyes opened fully. "You have water here?"

"This isn't a cave, Ms. Cross, despite what you may think of me." He bent over the bed, grasping her by the arms and pulling on them. "On your feet."

She stood, stretching, arms high. The blouse pulled up once more, and he watched the muscles of her tight belly flex, saw the way her breasts rose as she groaned the morning stiffness from her body.

"What do we need to do?" She fixed those brown eyes upon him as she rubbed her forearms, shivering. "This place is freezing."

"*We* don't need to do anything, but *you* need to strip those clothes off."

She laughed, shaking her head and rubbing her eyes. "Must be sleepy, still."

"You heard me." He crossed his arms, leaning a shoulder against the doorjamb once more. "Clothes off."

"Clothes... what?" She swallowed, her delicate little throat working. "Why?"

"Just do it." He lowered his voice. "Remember the discussion we had? About doing what you're told?"

"That didn't involve taking my clothes off in front of

you."

"It does now, Ms. Cross."

"You're fucking... no. Wait outside." She pointed toward the doorway, her slim finger trembling. "Please."

"No."

She made a frustrated sound, pulling down on the front of her blouse to hide her bare belly. "Let me go in the bathroom then, I'll hand you my clothes."

"No."

"Why not?" She backed up a step, deeper into the room, hugging herself.

"Defeats the purpose of checking you for a wire if I can't see you without your clothes, doesn't it?"

"What? Wire?" Her jaw clenched. "I'm not wearing a fucking wire... are you crazy? You *kidnapped* me. Why would I be wearing a wire?"

Lake shrugged. "You've proven so far that I can't trust you. And I'd be a goddamned idiot to trust your dad any farther than I could throw him. So I don't have a choice."

"Lake, I'm not. Seriously, this is... *please.*"

"The sooner you take off those clothes, the sooner you get that shower." He crossed one ankle over the other, enjoying her distress more than he'd imagined. "We've got all day, Ms. Cross."

"I can't..." Her eyes widened, her crestfallen expression almost bringing a smile to his face once more.

"You can, Ms. Cross — because you don't have any choice. Either you take off your clothes, or I'll take them off for you."

"Wait," she said, taking another step back. Lake followed, maintaining the distance. "You — you already saw me when"—her olive skin flamed with a blush—"when you, you *know.*"

"When I spanked you?" He smiled, shaking his head slowly. "I didn't see nearly enough, Ms. Cross. A wire can be tiny. God knows, I've rigged up enough of them in my life. Clothes. Off."

"You fucking *prick*."

"Maybe you need to go into that shower with a freshly whipped ass, too? I'm starting to think our meeting of the minds in the truck didn't really get through to you." He took another toward her, the floorboard creaking under his boot.

"No!" Her fingers worked at the buttons of her blouse. "I-I'm sorry. Please. Turn around or something? Do you have to watch?"

"Yes, I do. Stop stalling and get on with it."

He didn't, of course, but they both knew this was about a lot more than merely checking for a wire. She had a lot to learn and this was merely the first lesson. As he watched her eyes dart up to his, then slide away, her blush burning bright again, her true predicament was starting to dawn on her. This was really happening, and she was in no position to demand, or bargain.

Begging might get her somewhere though.

His cock was hard and throbbing by the time her fingers reached the last button, her chest rising in a deep, shaky breath. She looked up at him, tears welling in her brown eyes.

"Lake, *please*."

"Off, Ms. Cross. All of it." He took another step closer, clenching his jaw.

Her shoulders shuddered as she shrugged each arm out, letting the blouse fall to her feet. The lace of her bra matched the thong he'd seen in the truck, and for a moment he fought the urge to run a fingertip over the fabric, tease the tops of her breasts.

"Now the bra."

Her breath came fast, her breasts jiggling in the clutch of the black lace. Her dark hair drooped, hiding her face as she reached behind and unhooked the bra. It loosened and hung upon her bosom for a moment, a slight twist of her shoulders sending it tumbling, her hands instantly covering her breasts. She met his gaze, the defiance warring with her embarrassment.

"See? No wire."

"You aren't done. Get the rest of it off. I'm not going to tell you again, Ms. Cross."

"I-I can't do this." She looked down, shaking her head.

When he stepped closer to her, she froze, her whole body trembling even as she appeared to hold her breath. He was a mere foot away, and he could feel the heat of her body, the feminine scent of her mixed with her fear... and something else.

You're kidding yourself, Lake. She'd kick you in the nuts the first chance she got.

He traced a finger along her shoulder, stroking the silky skin at the hollow of her collarbone.

"Let's get this over with, Lily. It'll be quick."

She met his eyes then, confusion in those deep brown depths. It was a confusion he felt himself, twisting within him, unbalancing him. This was as new for him as it was for her.

You can't allow that, Lake. She'll use it against you, and you know it.

He stepped away, crossing his arms and giving her a harsh jerk of his chin toward the floor.

"Bastard," she said under her breath, working at the buttons of her jeans with one hand, the other arm crossed over her breasts.

"That smart mouth's going to cost you, Ms. Cross. But we'll take care of that later." He tilted his head. "First things first."

He let her wriggle herself out of those tight jeans with one hand, enjoying the sinuous movement of her hips as she struggled at the task.

"Don't forget the panties too."

"I hate you."

"I'm going to keep you alive, regardless. Stop stalling and get them off."

He was impatient to see her in all her glory, the fine

view of her ass still fresh in his mind. That she was a beauty was something he'd known from seeing her pictures, her dark hair and dusky skin set off with those big brown eyes. But having her here, alone, it had an effect on him he hadn't ever expected. She had such a will, a fiery spirit, and despite how much it aggravated him, that will only enhanced her beauty.

Having her here showed him something else though, a dark realization that filled him with anticipation, and — if he were brutally honest — a possessive, even sadistic, lust. He had an idea that he'd like to subjugate that will, bend it to his purposes, teach her to do what she was told. Taming that spirit — but not extinguishing it — held an appeal he couldn't quite articulate.

But he knew he'd like it. He'd like it very much indeed.

Her hand paused at the lace of her thong, her smooth thighs trembling ever so slightly. Lake felt a lump in his throat as he waited, not sure if she'd actually do it. Hoping she would — and hoping she wouldn't.

She hid behind the dark veil of her hair as she skimmed the thong down her legs, stepping out of it. For a moment, she stayed that way, crouched down, trying to protect the shred of modesty she had left, delaying the inevitable.

"I told you," she said, her voice soft. "No wire. Now let me get in the shower. Please."

"Stand up straight, Ms. Cross."

Rising, her eyes flashed, her delicate jaw clenching. One arm crossed over her breasts, her other hand covering her sex.

"You don't have to do this." Her voice broke, and she cleared her throat. "Why are you doing this? You know I don't have a wire, Lake."

"I'm doing this because I can't trust you, and because you need to learn how to do as you're told. Apparently, getting your ass tanned wasn't enough of a reminder for you." Lake shrugged. "That's fine. Plenty of other ways for me to get through to you. I'll keep trying them until I find one that works."

"I don't—"

"Keep that smart mouth shut." He stepped closer, his voice dropping to almost a whisper. "We could've gotten this done by now if you'd simply lowered your hands, but you had to push it. Every time you delay, every time you disobey, you'll regret it. Now, put your hands behind your head, and stand up straight."

"You... I can't."

"You can, and you will. Do I need to bind them behind your back? Do you want to try to wash yourself without the use of your hands?"

"No!" She dropped her head, taking a deep breath. "I'll... I'll do it. Fuck."

He had to suppress a smile as he watched her reluctantly rise to her full height, her movement almost slow motion. Then with a small, defeated sound, she brought her hands up to her head, her chin raised, mortification, defiance, and something indefinable warring within her gaze. Her lower lip quivered, and she clamped her teeth down upon it.

Taking a moment to look her over, he wished that time might slow, allow him to take it all in at his leisure. Her breasts weren't large, but rather were proportional to her slight frame, firm and high. The dark nipples had tightened into hard points, whether from mortification or something else, he couldn't tell.

He hoped it was both.

Her belly was tight and smooth, just like the rest of her, and he wondered what she did to keep that fit. Her overall physique suggested yoga, but then those strong thighs and round bubble butt made him think gymnast or some other sort of athlete. She was almost too trim though, the slight jut of her hip bones twin counterpoints to the deep navel, the smooth, elegant muscles of her belly. He wondered if she trained her body almost to the breaking point, relentless, uncompromising, to that pure state where there was only the exertion, her breathing, the pleasant fatigue of those muscles. More of that spirit that drew him to her, despite the surreal circumstances.

"We wouldn't have to do this if you'd listened. Remember that, Ms. Cross, next time you feel like you should be running the show here." He made sure he'd caught her gaze, before lowering his eyes to her bared sex. She kept it entirely smooth, the labia, like her bottom, surprisingly fleshy for one so slight, the lips of her sex closed in a tight seam that he wanted to tease with a fingertip, easing it between those folds to test that slippery heat.

Though he had no idea why, he knew she would be wet — despite the vitriol of her words, and the angry flash of her eyes. His cock wasn't the only thing at attention here.

"Are we done? Let me go, Lake."

"Turn around," he said, making the motion with an extended finger.

"Lake..."

He gave her an arch of his brow, his fingers drumming on his crossed arms.

"Maybe I need to stand there and supervise your shower too? Or do I need to wash you myself?"

"You'd like that, prick," she said under her breath as she turned, the slight movement of her hair matching the sway of her breasts

And then her ass was presented once more, and his breath caught in his throat. Her back tapered nicely down to twin dimples he found quite appealing indeed. Then the curve of her hips flared, bottom plump, lush even. The redness of her earlier spanking had disappeared almost entirely, only one spot, low on one cheek, threatening to darken with a small bruise. Her buttocks shivered a little as she shifted her weight, her fingers lacing tighter in that black mass of her hair.

"Legs shoulder-width apart."

Complying, she muttered something, but it was too

soft to make it out

"What was that, Ms. Cross?"

"Nothing... I. Please, isn't this enough?"

He reached up, clasping her hands in his, her body tensing. Her hair was soft against his knuckles, and he thought then how much he'd like to run his fingers through it, feel that silky weight in his palms.

Too close, Lake. She despises you anyway. Just be done with this.

"I want you to bend over now. Body parallel to the floor. Keep your hands where they are."

"Lake, for God's sake—"

He smacked her ass with a loud crack, and she jumped, yelping.

"I'm not telling you again, Ms. Cross."

She whimpered as she bent over, pausing a moment to widen her stance, hollowing her back and canting her hips a little to maintain her balance. Her movement was smooth, her hesitation borne of mortification rather than physical difficulty. He wondered at that as she held her position, the palm print blooming in deepening pink on her right buttock. The position was a stress position, intended to both expose the victim and physically tire them. He watched her for several long moments, the way the smooth thighs shivered with tension, the cords of the hamstrings taut, the crevice of her buttocks yawning open, the darkness within hinting at the anus not quite visible in the gathering morning light. The plump, smooth sex swelled below it, a glint of light catching what he'd suspected had gathered between the folds of her pussy. He laid a hand gently on her hip.

"Almost done."

Her response was half growl, half sob.

Crouching behind her, he stroked a hand up the inside of each thigh, gauging her reaction. Surprisingly, though her thighs tensed further, she didn't bolt, or even vocalize resistance. The handprint was an angry red now, and his palm caressed its heat before he ran his hands down her long, trembling thighs. This wasn't about the wire anymore, and he wanted her to know that, to get used to the fact that he could — and would — touch her anywhere he liked. The sooner she understood that she was under his control, the sooner she might settle down, and the sooner she might actually be able to *help* him keep both of their asses from ending their days in shallow graves.

"Spread your cheeks, spread everything."

Her breath caught at his words, and she froze. He could almost hear the wheels turning in her head, as she weighed the chances of punishment if she refused. He decided to help her along.

"If you don't, I will. And you won't like how I do it, either."

She cut off a small, desperate sob but her hands slipped back to cup her buttocks.

"Lake..."

He didn't respond, rather he let her dread — and his anticipation — hang heavy in the air. This was a turning point, of sorts. If he could get her to obey him here, he knew there was a glimmer of hope.

Her fingers grasped her cheeks and eased them slightly apart.

"More than that. I've got all day. Dragging it out only makes it worse for you."

Lily pulled them fully open, her back hitching once, a quavering sound from deep in her throat.

The dark whorl of her anus came into view, the perineum, the delicate petals of her inner lips visible between the plump lips of her sex. Unable to resist, he drew a fingertip between her buttocks, savoring the feel of the smooth flesh there. He tapped lightly on that tight, vulnerable entrance, and she grunted, her anus clenching reflexively.

"You know what to do, Ms. Cross."

Her fingers paused, one of them raised, shaking, as if

she were agonizing over the decision. He hoped she was.

Then those fingers moved lower, between the soft labia, splaying them, the bright wetness within making his cock throb once more.

"That's it." He turned his hand palm up and stroked a finger along that wet, pink flesh, the tip easing forward against the prominent hood protecting her clit. He worked that bundle of nerves for a moment, again curious at what she might do. He smiled at the involuntary tightening of her hamstrings and her harsh exhalation of breath, but, again, she stayed put.

"Interesting."

He rose, slapping her on the hip.

"Time for that shower."

She spun around immediately, her hands covering her sex and breasts once more. Her brow was furrowed, her teeth working at the corner of her mouth. She moistened dry lips with her tongue then took two deep breaths and looked up at him. But when he met her eyes, they weren't shooting daggers as he'd expected. He saw something else there instead.

Confusion.

She crouched down, reaching for her clothes.

"No. Those stay here. I need to check them too." He stepped back, sweeping an arm toward the door. "You're welcome to that shower now. You can close the door, but don't lock it."

"I don't... I don't understand this," she said, shouldering past him. "Any of it."

The door to the bathroom slammed, the springs of the mattress whispering as Lake sat down, studying the slippery moisture still glistening on his finger.

"Neither do I, Ms. Cross."

CHAPTER 7

In the time it took me to get into the bathroom, I was already blocking what had just happened from my mind. I looked at my face in the mirror. What the hell was wrong with me? I pushed the shower curtain aside, switched on the water and glanced at the lock on the door. I reached for the little button, knowing if he wanted to, he'd shove the damned thing open with his shoulder and punish me for locking it. I did it anyway though. I needed one minute where I could be alone, even if I was kidding myself.

The tile was cold beneath me but I sat there anyway, processing. I didn't believe my dad had hired Lake to protect me. Or rather, if he had hired Lake, Lake was no longer working for him. What had happened when he had knocked me out in the car? I had no idea and I wasn't sure I wanted to know. I did remember the feeling moments before though. And I remembered well DeSalvo pulling on his gloves, asking me something about what I'd be willing to do to survive.

A shiver ran through me and I rose up off the ground. What had happened a minute ago in that bedroom left no doubt as to how far I'd go to survive.

"Screw you, Lake Freeman!" It wasn't loud enough for him to hear and I did twist the doorknob a little to release the lock before I got into the shower. There was some noise in the hallway like he was drilling or something.

The water was thankfully hot, almost too hot, and the bathroom had already begun to steam up. I picked up the bottle of cheap shampoo and squeezed some onto my palm, scrubbing my head furiously.

What the fuck was that in the bedroom anyway? Checking me for a wire? Bullshit, and we both knew it. He was no different than other man — a horny fuck. He wanted to show me who was in charge? Well, I knew that. He hadn't had to make me do *that*.

And what about my reaction? Since when had I been one to strip when told to strip? Who dared even tell me to strip? Who dared tell me to bend over and…?

Heat flooded my face. *Fuck*! When had I forgotten who I was?

Blood boiled in my veins. At least I was getting angry. I might have been scared before, confused even. My body's reaction to him puzzled me but that was chemistry. That was all it was. And Lake could go fuck himself. He got himself an eyeful today. Probably was jerking off at the memory even now.

"Hope you enjoyed the view, Lake Freeman," I said aloud after rinsing my hair. I looked around for conditioner but all I found was a used bar of soap. Gross. My hair was going to be a wreck to comb through without conditioner.

Shaking my head, I switched off the water. I wasn't here to win a beauty contest. I was here because Lake Freeman had decided to kidnap me and bring me here. His intent? That I didn't understand. And quite frankly, I didn't care. I needed to get out of here. All I needed was a way out of the house, a few minutes to get to the truck and I'd be gone. Hell, maybe I could run him over on my way.

Two towels were stacked on a shelf in the corner. I wrapped my hair in one and dried off with the other before wrapping that one around myself, my clothes being in the other room where he could check them for a wire. Christ, what bullshit.

I opened the medicine cabinet but found only an expired bottle of Advil there.

"You about done in there?" Lake asked, knocking, making me jump.

"No."

I opened the drawers beneath the sink. There I found a toothbrush, some toothpaste and floss and one other thing that brightened my day a little: nail clippers, the old-fashioned kind with the file you could turn out that had the very sharp point. I could try to pick the lock on the window with it and if that failed, stabbing Lake was a good alternative. Better maybe.

He knocked on the door again and I palmed the clippers.

"What, you're knocking now?" I asked, my heart racing. What would he do if he caught me?

"You're right, I forgot myself," he said, his tone flat.

I pulled the towel tight around myself when he opened the door and looked me over.

"Get out," I said, meeting his gaze in the mirror.

"Mind your manners."

"Screw you."

"Lily..." he began, drawing out my name.

I needed a minute. "I need to brush my teeth. Can I at least get my toothbrush? I have one in my bag." I'd keep talking, distract him until I figured out what I was going to do. "And toothpaste. You know what, just get me my purse."

He raised his eyebrows. "I'm not your errand boy," he said. "Let's go, back in your room." He gripped my arm and pulling away was not an option. "I've got work to do."

"You've been busy already," I said, eyeing the brand new deadbolt on the outside of my bedroom door.

"If you prefer to be handcuffed to your bed, let me know. A little gratitude would go a long way, you know."

I looked at him, holding the towel tight to me, the clippers in the palm of my hand. I couldn't help myself. "So I should thank you for kidnapping me?" I asked, my smile saccharine. "Is that what you're waiting for? Is that why you've been acting like such a prick?"

"Careful, Lily. You get one warning."

Why my belly reacted like it did to that comment, I didn't even want to think about. I went into the room to find my purse there. It was open, and the contents had been dumped out onto the bed but it was here, at least. It was somehow a comfort.

"Be good, Lily," he said, pulling the door closed.

"Wait!" I called out, running to grab it.

He waited.

"What's happening?"

"Nothing. I have some things to do. You'll stay here while I do them." He began to pull the door closed.

"Are you leaving?" My tone was more panicked than I cared to admit.

"Are you going to miss me?" he asked, leaning against the doorframe.

"You're an asshole."

"Didn't think so. Be good, or else."

"Screw you."

His expression changed and his hand was around my throat in an instant, walking me back into the room and holding me against the wall. I curled my hand around his forearm trying to pull him off while my other hand fisted against his chest, his rock-hard chest, reminding me that there was one person in charge here and it wasn't me.

"I'm sorry," I managed quickly, a part of me reacting, surviving maybe, deciding to bow down without my permission.

He stared at me for a full minute before his hand loosened a little. He looked like he wanted to say something but then changed his mind and released me. Without another word, he walked out the door. It was when I heard the deadbolt sealing me in that I realized I was holding my breath.

My entire body trembled as I lowered myself onto the bed. I went to the window and pushed the curtains aside. Shutters from the outside kept the room dark. I tried to push the window open but wasn't surprised to find it locked. I set the clippers down and quickly pulled on my clothes that he had piled on the bed. Once dressed, I took the clippers and got to work on the lock.

I'd never done anything like this before and that was fairly obvious when I tried to stick the thing into the lock. It always looked easy in the movies, but this was reality. It didn't take a brain surgeon to figure out this wasn't going to be my exit.

"Crap."

I touched my thumb to the point of the file. After all he had done to me, I didn't want to do this to him. It was too close, too personal, too…violent.

What about what he did to you?

Close, personal and violent would about cover that. I had to get my shit together. When he opened that door and came in here, I'd have to do it. I'd have to do it fast, surprise him and run the hell out of here. I'd use his own deadbolt to lock him in here then get in the truck and go.

Go where though? The US Marshal was ready to hand me over to Randall. Randall was out looking for me, I could bet my life on that. The police? Idiots. And the ones who weren't idiots could be bought.

My dad was set to testify in the next few months. I was only of use to Randall until then. I'd just have to hide out for a little while. That was doable. And I'd have to get word to my dad that I was okay.

But first, I had to get out of here.

I picked up my bag and felt inside it, touched the very bottom where the cash and my key to the safe deposit box were hidden, relieved to see he'd not found the secret pocket.. I only needed to make sure to grab my bag when I bolted.

It would only be a few months. There was an end in sight and I could do this on my own.

I lay down on the bed and stared up at the ceiling, thinking of what had happened just before my shower. I'd been with men before, not a lot but I wasn't a virgin either. But what he had made me do, that was something different. I should have been disgusted by it, ashamed, humiliated. But I wasn't; there was no room for that. Instead, I slid my hand over my belly and unbuttoned my jeans. The zipper came down next and my fingers slid into my panties, over my bare sex, finding my already swollen, wet clit. A sound came from my throat and I rolled over onto my belly, pressing my face into the pillow. My fingers worked that hard little nub fast, the memory of standing there like I had, the image of myself bent over, spreading myself. The feel of his fingers on me, on my clit, my pussy, my asshole.

I swallowed, the sound loud, the pillow wet when I pressed my thighs together, pushing hard against my clit, rubbing into the mattress, hips bucking, my fingers soaked.

I stayed like that for a long time afterward, my eyes open, staring at a white wall wondering what the hell was wrong with me that the image of myself bending over and spreading myself open on my kidnapper's order could get me off.

I tightened my hold on the clippers that were now under my pillow, pulled my hand out of my jeans and waited.

* * *

It was a long time before I heard him at the door. I had fallen asleep at some point and sat up fast now, wiping sleep from my eyes, suddenly very alert, my sorry weapon in hand.

What if it didn't work? He'd be mad. No, he'd be pissed.

No time for doubt. I had one chance.

I stood then sat back down. The lock slid and I watched the doorknob turn. I needed him to come inside. If I waited at the door, he'd know something was up. Hell, I'd be lucky if he didn't know the second he opened the door as it was.

My purse! It was beside the bed on the floor. Okay, it was okay. I could do this. I just had to breathe and stay calm.

"Hope you've been a good girl, Lily," Lake said, pushing the door open and walking inside.

I stared up at him and he stared back. Something passed through his eyes and he glanced around the room. This was it. Without allowing myself to even think about it, I ran at him, the sharp point of the file aimed straight at him, straight at his neck.

For a split second, he looked surprised.

But I hesitated. I was inches from him and I hesitated so when I finally moved to stab him, he caught my wrist and leaned to the side so I stabbed air instead. My free hand scratched at his face, trying for his eyes but he caught that one too, pushing me back, looking at me for a moment, his eyes hard, taking the clippers from me before pushing me onto the bed.

He looked at what he held. "Nail clippers, Lily?" he asked, laughing but not really. "Fucking nail clippers?"

He stalked toward me and I climbed backward on the bed, feeling tears on my face but not knowing when I'd started crying. "I'm sorry!" He grabbed my arm hard, yanking. "I'm sorry, Lake!"

His eyes were so dark, all I could do was stare up at

him, my body trembling.

He made a sound and let go of me. Without a word, he walked out of the room, and slid the deadbolt back into place.

CHAPTER 8

Lake paced the front porch, needing the invigorating chill of the fresh air, his mind a mass of confusion, disappointment, and, oddly, excitement. He knew even going outside at all was dangerous at this point, but he didn't have a choice.

The complication inside the house had just gotten a helluva lot more complicated.

Fishing his phone out of his jeans pocket, he punched the number, kicking the base of one of the roof pillars of the porch, white paint flaking off onto the black leather of his boot.

"Kellen." A pause, and a quiet chuckle. "Freeman, where the fuck have you been?"

"Shut up and listen. I'm gonna need you on this right away. Drop whatever you're doing."

"Okay, this should be good." Kellen's deceptively laconic voice was muffled for a minute then he was back on. "I'll need twenty minutes to kit then I'll be rolling."

"You remember where you picked us up?"

"Yep."

"I left the car in a quarry, half a click from our pickup. You think you can find it?"

Kellen gave him a dramatic sigh. "Bailing your ass out again, aren't I?"

"Will need a clean. Four-door sedan. I tucked the keys inside the front bumper, driver's side corner." Lake lowered the phone, thumbs whirling over the screen, then put it back to his ear. "You should have the location in a second."

"Got it. Disposal, too?"

"Nope. Leave it be." Lake glanced back at the closed door. "He'll be back for it, I have no doubt. He's gotta keep his shit wired tight just as much as I do."

"Press?"

"Would *you* want to be the first US Marshal in history to lose a person from WITSEC?"

Kellen chuckled. "Poor bastard. Shitting himself right about now."

"I wish that were true." Lake's voice lowered. "I did some checking on him. He's a heavy hitter. I got lucky, actually."

"Nothing Kell can't handle, boss."

"I mean it, Kellen. Quick and simple — then get the fuck out of there. And stay gone for a while. He'll have help now."

"I should have it done in four hours, six if you left a mess."

"I didn't, dickhead."

"And just when I thought the day was getting interesting."

Kellen hung up.

Lake stared out at the trees swaying in the stiff breeze, inhaled the fresh scent of the forest. He'd missed this place, missed the quiet, the clean air, the solitude. He reached up, curling his fingertips over the top of the beam that spanned the porch, stretching his tense shoulders.

"Are you really doing this?" he whispered.

The images that played out in his mind had his groin tightening. Her gorgeous body, her silence, the trembling of her limbs as she'd reluctantly obeyed him. Perhaps such thoughts made him a bastard at best, a monster at worst. His physical reaction was true though, regardless of morals, of right or wrong. She needed to understand this, the truth of it, to get it through her head just how deep she was here. Her behavior couldn't be tolerated, and allowing her any more leeway — or leniency — was now out of the question. First, there was the near disaster at the rest stop, and now the idiotic, almost comical stunt with the nail clippers.

Nail clippers.

Did she think this was a fucking movie?

Yes, he *was* doing this. He was going to teach her — and she was going to learn, whether she wanted to or not.

And he was going to enjoy it.

* * *

Originally, he'd built it as a guest room, separated from the main house. But after he'd built it, he'd never used it. The bathroom was still unfinished, and although it did have a modest bedroom set, it had become essentially a shed.

It took him longer than he'd anticipated to move everything out, transferring most of the tools, the extra blankets, and furniture to the garage. By the time he'd finished, he was sweating, so he shed his jacket, the dark T-shirt wet against his chest. He checked the door latches and the locks, and other than being a little sticky from disuse, they checked out. His fingers tested the steel D-rings set along one of the walls. Years ago, once he'd resigned himself to the likelihood that no actual people would be staying in the room, he'd had the rings installed, intending to use them to string chain along the wall in order to store all the tools upright and secure.

Now, they'd finally be used for their intended application — but it wouldn't be tools he'd be securing.

Making his way back into the house, he tiptoed down the hall, knowing exactly where the creaks in the floor were. He slid the deadbolt on her door silently, easing the door open. She lay motionless, on her back, her hair a tangled mass of silky black. For a moment, he thought she might be sleeping, but when he shut the door, she sprang up with a startled yelp, hugging her knees to her chest, her dark gaze watching him. He pondered what thoughts might be flitting behind those eyes, if she wondered what was going to happen to her next. Lake was sure she had no idea. Truth be told, he wasn't even sure himself — but the ideas were coming together, and fast.

Her feet were bare, their pale vulnerability fetching in its own confusing way. He *liked* her vulnerability, because it made him want to exploit it and yet, at the same time, it elicited a twisted urge to protect her.

From himself.

He pointed at her, lifting his finger, beckoning her to

stand.

Those dark eyes stared back, unreadable, her arms clutching her knees tighter.

Lake moved closer, standing over her. For a moment, he simply looked down upon her, feeling the excitement build within him at having her so close. Where once she'd irritated him, had made him want to push her away, now it was something else entirely. He hadn't thought of any of this, of course, back there in that car. The possibilities that stretched before him, her fate determined by a simple choice of paths, by a split second decision. No, when he'd heard DeSalvo speak the words that made had Lake's blood run cold, there wasn't time for any of that. There was only time to protect her, to save her.

But was it really to save her? Or was it to keep her for himself? Was he snatching her from the jaws of one monster, only to carry her away to another? Twelve hours ago, he'd have laughed at such a question. But now, as he watched how her body trembled ever so slightly, the way her eyes followed him, their depths keen, unblinking, he wasn't so sure.

Reaching for her, he eased a palm against her cheek, and she jerked her head away, an angry sound in her throat. He clutched her chin, squeezing, pain clouding her gaze. Tilting her face up to his, he stared into her eyes.

"Ow! What the fu—"

His finger wagged before her, admonishing.

"You've proven you're not worthy of being trusted, Lily. So we're going to start over at the beginning. First rule: no speaking, unless I ask you a direct question. Nod if you understand."

"I understand you're a fucking psycho."

"That's what I thought."

Lake clamped a hand on her upper arm and hauled her off the bed, sending her sprawling. Her legs scrambled for purchase on the carpet as he turned for the door, dragging her by the arm. She was so light, he felt as if he could've slipped her right into his pocket if he'd chosen to. But she needed this too, needed to know that physically she was utterly outmatched and that any resistance would entail consequences. Painful ones.

"Let me go!" she yelled as he steadily drew her behind him down the hallway toward the living room. "Jesus, just let me — I'll follow...Goddammit!"

He opened the front door, and turned back to her.

"You can walk out there, or I can walk you out. It's your choice."

"Where are you — where are we going?"

Lake tipped his head toward the front window, and her gaze followed. Seeing what lay beyond, her eyes shot open.

"No. *No!*" She pulled against his grip, hard. "Not there."

"Guess there's my answer."

Lake hauled her off her feet with ridiculous ease, clutching her tightly in his arms, squeezing a gasp from her as she flailed against him. She cursed, her body twisting within his grip, a trail of hot pain flaming along his neck as her nails raked his skin. He caught her wrist and squeezed until she cried out.

"You're going to pay for that one too, Lily."

"Let me go! I'll do what you want." Her voice spiraled higher. "No — don't do it. Please."

"Oh yes, you're going all right. You've earned it."

He paused a moment then headed back toward the kitchen, his hand around Lily's wrist. She pulled hard, slowing him for a moment, then he yanked her forward, and she stumbled after him, her bare feet clapping loudly on the floorboards. He pulled open one of the drawers in the kitchen, the wood screeching in its carriage. He'd need to grease that later, once he'd gotten this over with.

Once he had some peace and quiet.

Rummaging around in the drawer, he pulled out the tape. Using his teeth to unroll a piece, he looked at Lily.

"I'm letting you go for one second. Don't move or

you're going into that room with a freshly whipped ass."

"You'll whip me anyway, you prick."

"Probably, but it'll be worse for you if you try it. Don't, Lily."

Then he let go, fully expecting her to bolt. Incredibly, she didn't. Rather, she stood in that kitchen, rubbing her wrist, her gaze shocked, disbelieving, the whites of her eyes showing as she watched him tear loose the piece of duct tape.

Then something seemed to come over her, her eyes narrowing, and she whirled so quickly, she almost slipped out of his reach. His fingers clenched on a handful of her shirt below the nape as she lunged back toward the living room. The ripping sound of the shirt tearing was loud in the small kitchen, and she slowed for only a split second. It was all he needed.

She screeched as his fingers twisted into her long hair and pulled back, her arms wind milling in front of her as he hauled her off balance. She tumbled backward, twisting in his grip, and he dropped down to a knee next to her as she sprawled on the floor, her knee thudding against the floorboard

"Lake! No pl—"

He slapped the tape over her lips, a long lock of hair caught at the corner of her mouth, then flipped her over onto her chest, her gasp a whooshing sound as the impact with the floor knocked the wind out of her. She wheezed, twisting like a landed fish, grunting as he wrapped more tape around her wrists, binding them at the small of her back. She finally sucked in a great gust of air as he yanked her back to her feet, her eyes wild, her words hopelessly muffled by the tape. Her shirt hung askew, torn at the neckline, the upper curve of a breast exposed.

"You could've cooperated. But we'll have it your way instead." He pointed back into the living room. "Now move."

She refused to walk, so he caught a fistful of her hair

close to her scalp, twisting a little, making her whine, until her feet started to move. He frog-marched her out the front door and into the chilly late afternoon air. She tried to say something, her tone plaintive, but he ignored it, kicking the door to the guest room open and walking her inside. Lily jerked as he slammed the door shut behind them.

He let her see what he'd laid out on the bed before spinning her toward the wall and pushing her against it, his hand splayed between her shoulder blades. She tried to push back, but he pressed more of his weight against her, and she stilled.

"Stop this, Lily," he growled. "You're not going to win. Just stop, for Christ's sake."

There was a note of exasperation in his voice, even as his cock was a throbbing iron spike in his pants. He didn't even want to think about why this was turning him on so much.

From one monster to the next. Right, Lake?

She whimpered as he placed the blindfold over her eyes, ensuring it fit snugly, with no gaps. A hood would have worked better, but it wasn't time for that. Not yet, anyway.

Grasping a fistful of her hair, he swung her around and threw her over the bed, her legs hanging over the side, her bare toes scrabbling against the dusty floor. He inserted a knee between her legs, forcing them apart as he knelt on the mattress, straddling one of her thighs. Plucking the knife from the mattress, he deftly sliced through the tape at her wrists. The metal touched her skin, and Lily froze, a scared note to the sounds coming from behind the tape.

"Afraid, Lily?" There was no way in hell he'd ever cut her, but she didn't need to know that, especially if that fear might get her to comply for a change.

I don't think you want her to comply, Lake. What would be the fun in that? Monster.

He shook his head with a curse, dropping the blade to

the mattress again and grabbing the leather cuffs. Wrapping each wrist in the thick leather, he attached the metal snap, linking them securely together behind her back. She yanked against them instantly, her fight not even close to extinguished.

"You're not getting out of them until I let you out, so you might as well quit. You'll just tire yourself out." She squealed, rage in her voice, and Lake shook his head. "Or not."

Catching each of her waving legs in turn, Lake clasped the delicate ankles in thick leather too, pulling the manacles snug. He'd need to check the circulation in those toes a little later. He let her feet down again, her legs a straight, pleasing line from the edge of the mattress down to the floorboards.

He looked her over a moment, weighing options, what to do next. With the cuffs on, there was no other way. And it might get through to her the way nothing else had thus far.

Lake brought the blade to Lily's neck, moving aside the mass of her hair, pressing the metal to her skin. She froze instantly.

"You don't have any other clothes, do you, Lily? Nod for yes, shake your head for no."

She shook her head slowly.

"Good."

The blade made quick work of the arms of her blouse, but rather than cut the fabric, Lake indulged his caveman urges and ripped it from the neckline all the way to her waist. He threw the tattered remnants aside, working the sharp knife under the shoulder straps of her brassiere then down the fabric at the clasp before ripping the bra away too, Lily grunted loudly as her body jostled.

"Had you cooperated, you'd still be in the bedroom," Lake said, the blade slicing through one leg of her jeans, from ankle all the way up and over the swell of her buttock. Then he sliced down from the waist, his fingers brushing against the soft flesh of her ass as the jeans gave way. "Instead, you chose to disobey me again. Now, you've lost both your clothing and your freedom."

I don't think she's been free since you kidnapped her, Lake.

Her soft buttocks wobbled as he pulled the destroyed jeans from underneath her, and she whimpered once more. His fingers insinuated under the lace of her thong, and he ripped it from her body, the sound firing his lust once more, the surprised cry from behind the tape making him smile, despite himself.

Then Lake eyed the pillows piled at the head of the bed and the two implements still lying across the mattress next to the rapidly breathing and very naked Lily. The lush, round buttocks had broken out in goose flesh, and he smoothed a palm over them to feel the texture of it, to feel the fright in her trembling flesh. His hand eased between the tightly clenched thighs, fingertips whispering down the thin line between her smooth legs.

His fingers traced over the stiff brown leather of the paddle, tracing the four letters burned into the center of it. He moved to the long, supple leather strap next to it, the end cut into two hard-edged tongues that he knew would bite like fire when wielded with a will. He wondered which one the girl needed, which one he wanted to give her.

And as he stood there adjusting the huge erection twisting in his jeans, he wondered if he'd lost his mind.

* * *

The only sound I heard was that of my own heart beating at a frantic pace, my own breathing loud from inside my chest. The blindfold was wet, and I thought if he took the tape off my mouth, I'd vomit, my throat felt so full, like I was going to choke on fear.

Fear.

I couldn't stop shaking, my body an earthquake, and when I splayed out my hands to cover my bottom, my fingers brushed his and I pulled them back, adrenaline forcing action from me, forcing me to cry out from behind the tape and try one more time, just once more, to get away from him, even as I knew how hopeless, how pathetic the effort was.

"Now, now, Lily," he said, gripping my thigh hard enough to hurt while his voice maintained a calm that told me he had a plan, that he'd given this some thought. "You asked for this remember," he said, setting what I knew to be the strap I'd seen before he had blindfolded me onto my shoulder. The leather was so close to my face, I could smell it, and when he began to drag the weight of it slowly down my back, I did cover my ass with my hands.

"That won't do at all," he said.

His hands worked and in a moment, my own were free. Confused, I fought his grip. He let them go for one instant, flipping me onto my back, and when he did, even with my ankles bound, I brought my knees up to fight him, clawing at whatever part of him I could get close to. He made a sound, a grunt, and I knew I'd hurt him at least a little, but I knew at the same time that the hurt he would do to me would be ten times that, a hundred times.

Pushing my legs flat, he straddled me and my wrists were quickly re-bound in the cuffs. I stopped then, out of breath, out of fight and he patted my face, saying something I didn't quite hear. I squeezed my eyes shut thinking he might slap me but he didn't. Instead, I was flipped back over onto my stomach, but this time, he took my arms and stretched them toward the headboard and I heard something click into place. When his hands left mine, I tugged only to find myself trapped, the cuffs locked to something either against the headboard or the wall, I didn't know which. He pulled me down toward the foot of the bed and my legs dangled off until they too were linked and I was effectively stretched, my legs half on the bed, half off.

The bed creaked when he stood. "There," he said, still somehow calm. I imagined him standing back, watching me, taking in every naked inch of my bound, stretched body.

My own breathing came fast then as the full realization of my vulnerability dawned on me. I think I was trying to beg then. Tears were coming fast and I pleaded for him not to hurt me, begged his forgiveness from behind the tape.

"What's that, Lily?" he asked, tugging the pillows out from under my arms and pressing them beneath my hips, lifting my ass higher. "I'm sorry. I can't quite understand you."

His words seemed to come from some distant place. I was so caught up in what I knew was coming, what I knew there was no way out of. I wanted to go back to that little bedroom. My room. I wanted out of here.

"What did you say?" he asked again.

He patted the strap against my ass, taking aim. I pulled ankles and wrists, frantic to free myself, managing to push the blindfold askew at least off one eye. I looked ahead at the dark wall through the metal rungs of the headboard, saw the ring he'd clipped the cuffs to. I turned my head in time to see him swing his arm hard, his eyes on mine as I screamed from behind the tape when the leather seared a stripe of pure fire across my ass.

"How's that, Lily?" he asked, patting the strap against my ass again.

Another scream before he even struck, the pain forcing tears from my eyes. I'd never felt anything like this before.

This pain was unreal.

He didn't wait this time, laying another punishing stroke down at the juncture between my bottom and my thighs. I tensed every muscle, squeezing my legs together, clenching my buttocks tight. Another stroke, this one dead center.

"You know what?" he asked, pausing, coming toward me, the weight of one knee depressing the mattress by my face. "I think," he began as he adjusted the blindfold over my eyes once more, "I might like to hear the sound of your screams." He pulled the tape painfully from my mouth, causing more hot tears from my eyes.

"Please, Lake. Please..."

"You don't have to beg me, honey," he said, moving behind me again. "I know what you need."

I heard the sound of the strap coming this time and clenched everything tight in anticipation, but it didn't diminish the pain, not even a little. My scream filled the room and I hadn't quite absorbed the sound of it before another stroke burned my ass.

I was going to die. He was going to kill me. I was convinced of it as stroke after stroke fell covering the whole of my bottom, the tops of my thighs. He seemed untiring while I screamed until I had nothing left, no voice, no breath, only pain, absolute pain.

If he thought he hadn't made his point, he was dead wrong.

"That's it," he said, a hand slapping my ass hard, the different sensation causing me to jump to attention. "Lie there and take your punishment. Ten more."

"Please. It's enough. I promise I'll be good. I'm sorry. I'm so sorry." The blindfold was drenched and I wiped my face against my arm. Sweat covered me, the heat of my punished flesh degrees hotter than anything else.

He rubbed my bottom, his touch almost soft as he covered both mounds. I thought he'd changed his mind. I thought, as I listened to his breathing calm, that he took pity on me, that it was over. But then he stopped rubbing and stepped back.

"Count them."

My sobbing took on a whole new meaning then. He wouldn't stop, not until he'd delivered every last one of those ten strokes and it wouldn't matter what I said, how much I cried or begged, how raw he whipped my ass. He would do this; there would be no mercy. Not today, not any day. Not with him. He was teaching me.

I shuddered as the first of the final ten landed.

"Lily," he urged, drawing out the way he said my name. "I'll keep going until you count."

"One!"

"Good girl. Now keep your ass nice and soft for me. Relax your muscles. Soft. That's it. Be good."

His words were almost gentle but the leather unforgiving, cruel even. I called out the count every time, tried to relax my muscles every time he reminded me to and took the last of the strokes. And when it was done, I went limp, weeping into my arms, soaking the bed with my tears.

The strap landed on the floor with a thud but I remained as I was. He didn't speak and when his fingertips grazed my ass, I flinched but didn't pull away. His touch felt strange, not good, I was too tender for that, but it somehow reassured? It made no sense but all I could do was remain as I was, and when he pulled my cheeks apart, I tensed but only for a moment. He spread me open and I swallowed, grateful suddenly for the blindfold, grateful not to have to look at him as he surely looked at me, at my most private places. My face burned with shame while his fingers moved between my bottom cheeks and grazed the open lips of my pussy before trailing higher, circling my back hole.

But that was all and I don't know if I was grateful or not when he stopped.

He freed my legs both from the thing I'd been bound

to and the cuffs that kept my ankles together. He left my arms as they were but I was able to draw my knees up, tucking them underneath my hips, crawling slowly, painfully onto the bed, my burning ass high in the air, not caring what I looked like.

"There," he said, rolling me onto my side. "Punishment is over." He lifted my head onto his lap and with the gentlest touch, removed the blindfold. "Shh…" he coaxed, fingers pushing the hair off my wet face. "I hope you learned your lesson, Lily," he said. "I hope you'll not make me punish you like this again."

I looked up at him through wet lashes, the image of him blurred.

We stayed like that for a while, him looking at me, touching my face, brushing my hair back coaxing me to stop crying, and in time, I did. I stopped and my breathing slowly returned to normal but throughout that time, however long it was, I couldn't *not* look at him. What I felt I don't know. I didn't have a word for it. What I saw in his eyes, well, that too was indescribable. They were dark, darker than usual and when he slowly moved to stand, I made a sound. It wasn't any word, simply sound, but he understood my meaning even when I could not. He stayed as he was, kept my head on his lap, caressed my shoulder and slowly turned me onto my back. I groaned when my bottom made contact with the rough blanket but I didn't fight him. Perhaps I *had* learned to obey.

"Open your legs," he said.

I searched his face but his eyes only urged me to do as he said and I did, and when I did, I watched his gaze slide over me, over my breasts, my belly, down to my sex. His throat worked as he swallowed and this time when he moved to stand, I didn't make a sound but held my breath instead. He went to the foot of the bed, his eyes intent on my sex which, somehow, even with the pain on my backside, even knowing that he was the one who inflicted that torture on me, somehow, with his eyes on me, a different sort of heat consumed all of my attention and when he knelt between my legs, I didn't move. I didn't close them or cry out or anything. I simply remained watching him and Lake took hold of my thighs and pushed them wider, his eyes hungry, never once leaving that space as he brought his mouth to it, soft and wet and hot and when his lips closed over my clit, I sucked in a breath and a new wave of crying consumed me, the sensations of softness so opposite the punishment of moments before carrying me to a place where a throbbing heat coupled with that of absolute pleasure drew a cry from my lips.

My eyelids closed and I lifted to him, opening for him. His tongue worked and his fingers slid into me, the days-old scruff on his face the only thing rough against my pussy, and when he sucked my clit, I came harder than I'd ever come before. My breath caught and a moan from deep inside me filled my ears. His mouth, his hot, wet, soft mouth connected to me. It was all consuming and when my hips stopped bucking and I opened my eyes again, I watched him rise from the bed. I watched him watch me, watched him wipe the back of his hand across his mouth. The thick length of his cock pressed against his jeans, and for a moment, I wasn't sure what was next, what I wanted, what he would do.

Then, without a single word, he was gone, leaving me bound to the bed. I closed my legs, pressing my thighs together, squeezing the still-tender nub, and rolled over onto my stomach. I could still feel him on me, feel his mouth closed over me, and, rubbing my swollen clit against the rough cover of the bed, I came again before falling asleep, bound, alone, and shivering, the sweat from my punishment now a cold layer of moisture over my body.

CHAPTER 9

Lake brought the axe down on the wood, splitting it cleanly, one half of the log flipping end over end off to the side, the other half staying utterly still, as if it had always been thus, had always been whole.

Though he already had at least five cords of wood stacked along the side of the house, Lake needed to do this. He needed the exertion, the distraction from the turmoil of his mind. This was simple; this made sense. It had purpose. Necessary or not, there was a *reason* for this.

What had just happened in that guest room had no purpose. There wasn't a fucking reason in the galaxy for what he'd done. He dropped the blade onto a knot-filled log, the steel catching fast. He stooped to pick up the wedge, laying it against the rusted blade. The sledgehammer struck it once, twice, Lake grunting as he hit it harder a third time, driving the wedge through.

He was already sweating.

The line had been there — that unspoken, ephemeral, yet concrete point of no return.

And he'd fucking obliterated it.

Yet. as he placed another log on the broad stump, raised his axe once more, his calmness remained. He should have been worried, should have been ashamed.

But he wasn't. Not in the least.

It was her reaction that had sent everything spinning off axis, if only for a moment, that most unexpected thing, and yet the most welcome. A relief, a moment of respite in this twisted journey he'd embarked upon, the helpless, beautiful, forlorn Lily in tow.

It still didn't make sense. Was it biology? A defense mechanism? He'd studied it, of course. He'd even put it into practice in SERE training. Resist, in whatever way, whenever you could. Even the tiniest resistance was so important, for it focused the mind, fended off despair, and worse, shock.

Of course, she couldn't know that; he doubted Lily would've survived a single day of basic training, let alone Special Forces training. But she had that fire, that instinct to survive, that not all people really knew how to tap into. And she was strong, stronger than he'd ever suspected.

That still didn't explain it though. She'd actually had an *orgasm.*

At first, he'd simply been too shocked to react to it, the earthy scent of her on his lips, the taste of her still upon his tongue. He'd thought to simply punish her, and punish her he had.

Lying there with her afterward though, he wondered what she was thinking, why she fought at every turn.

Because she senses what you are inside.

Did she fight because of that knowledge, or had she *come* because of that knowledge? What if the two were becoming as confused for her as his role was becoming to him?

That wasn't quite true, either, though. Lake stretched, dropping the axe to the turf and taking a seat on the stump, the splinters prickly but tolerable through the protection of his jeans. The smell of the pitch from the split wood rose around him, the clean, spicy scent of it making him smile. The memory of cutting wood as a child, when his dad had first taught him how to swing an axe, came back to him. It was a time when his father would've been proud of him — and when all Lake had ever wanted was the approval of his father.

Now, that Lake was gone.

When he thought of Lily again, the confusion welled within him once more. How was it possible? Could she? Did she? Questions piled one on top of the other, the answers drowned out by the conflict within him at where he now stood. He examined what he felt, why he felt, and although that small, quiet voice still whispered, it was faint. So faint.

He'd see this through, see where it led, even if the final destination was a place he could not go, an end he would not choose for her.

Lake leaned over onto one hip, fishing his cell from his pocket, wiping a bead of sweat from his temple. The birds in the trees behind him began their singsong serenading again as he looked at the phone, frowning at it.

No message on the clean, yet.

It didn't mean anything, of course. Kellen wasn't exactly known for being talkative. He seemed more like a ghost than a man. Lake didn't even know where his partner was half the time. Which was probably a good thing.

Distracting yourself won't change anything.

Lake stood, groaning at the heavy soreness in his testicles. He hadn't come, hadn't allowed what his body had been screaming for as he'd had her under his tongue, her enticing scent all around him. The thought had him hardening all over again, regardless of the new pain flaring in his balls.

"Fuck," he muttered, wiping the splinters from the seat of his jeans, taking one last deep breath of the clean scent of the woods, the waning evening light still warm on his skin.

It was time for some ground rules. And it was time to see how deep he wanted to take her.

* * *

The nude body stirred as he closed the door behind him, the darkness deepening as the evening light waned outside. For a moment, he stood there, watching her watch him, her eyes bright in the gathering shadows. He was pleased she didn't try to speak, pleased that she seemed to be learning after all.

"I'm going to untie your hands, but I know you won't try anything, will you?" He dropped his gaze pointedly to the strap still lying on the floorboards, waiting, like a black serpent.

Lily shook her head, her eyes widening.

"Good."

He untied the cuffs from the headboard, then unclipped them from one another, allowing her to move her hands independently. She groaned as she flexed her shoulders, rubbing the backs of her arms.

"Hurting? You can speak."

"Yes. Arms are killing me. You…"

"Go on."

"You left me like that…too long."

"You weren't going anywhere." He pointed to the headboard. "But that was to make sure you knew it."

He sat down on the foot of the bed, her eyes watching him the whole time. He merely looked at her, taking in the movement of her naked breasts as she kneaded one arm, her elbow folded across her chest in a futile effort to conceal her breasts.

"That's another of your rules. Never cover yourself, Lily."

She stopped, lowering her arms haltingly until her hands clasped her bare thighs. Her breathing was already increasing, the rise and fall of her chest coming faster now.

"And what was your first rule?"

"Don't speak — unless spoken to." Her voice was rough, almost hoarse. Considering how loud she'd been screaming, he was surprised she'd had any voice left at all.

"Good, you remembered." He turned toward her,

resting his thigh along the mattress, his leg crossed over the other one. "But you forgot something."

The crease of her brow and the quiver of her lower lip almost made him smile.

"Relax. I'm not going to punish you. I haven't told you this one yet."

The set of her shoulders eased a little.

"When you speak to me, you address me as 'Sir.' Always."

"Yes…Sir."

He smiled at her then. "You're on a roll, Lily girl."

Lily's stomach growled loud and long, her cheeks coloring.

"Hungry?"

"Yes, Sir."

Lake scratched his chin. "Well, if you're good, maybe we can get you something to eat. But first it's time to see if you've learned how to do as you're told."

Her big eyes watched him, her teeth worrying her lip again.

"I want you to stand up and walk over to that wall." He pointed to the wall next to the bed. "Face it and wait."

He thought she'd resist it, and he sighed as he waited, moving his hand along the mattress in the direction of the paddle that still lay there.

Finally, she rose and turned to the wall, looking at him over her shoulder before facing it, her head bowed, her hands clenched to fists at her sides.

Her bottom looked swollen, the rounded perfection of her buttocks marred by broad marks, faded to a deep pink from the livid red welts he'd watched the strap leave across her pale skin. The marks across her thighs, though, were more inflamed, a bluish bruise already darkening along one of the stripes.

"Do you see those rings in the wall above you? Reach up and grab one."

She looked up then glanced at him over her shoulder

again.

"Eyes front, Lily. Do as you're told."

With a little shudder, her arms reached up, her shoulder blades slowly moving as her body stretched. She had to go up on her toes to reach it, the smooth muscles of her calves bunching as she rose. Her fingers curled around the metal, and she stilled, a lock her hair falling down her back, the darkness of it contrasting against the clear smoothness of her skin.

For long moments he simply sat there, watching her, his heart pounding with the same painful throbbing of his hard cock. The delicate muscles of her arms stood tight, her position emphasizing the slenderness of her ribcage, the trim waist, the swell of that round, heart-shaped ass that called to the predator in him, called for both caresses and lashes. Her strong, lithe thighs trembled as she strained upward, the bruise deepening more, the color making him want to kiss it, to trace that line of pain with gentle, possessive fingers.

Every second he watched her seemed an eternity, his lust rising until all he could think about was falling upon her helpless body, taking from her what he knew he had no right to take. Yet he knew now that her body wanted him to take it anyway, even if her mind fought it, fought him — and what surrendering to him might mean. Right and wrong, good or evil, none of that mattered now. There was only lust, the animal rising within him. For too long he'd suppressed this side of himself. He'd wondered if it had died with his wife. But, as he took in the pale, smooth lines of Lily's stretched, trembling form, he knew the truth of things, and the realization was both a joy and a sorrow. How could he be what he really was? How could she—

Stop it, Lake. Just feel. Just be.

Up on his feet and advancing, he reached her in two steps, wrapping a hand in her hair, making her gasp. His other hand clasped her throat, squeezing just enough to make her still, her pulse pounding against his fingers, her breath coming in rapid little pants.

"Tell me something, Lily. What were you, when you were younger?" He released her throat, easing his hand down her back to cup the soft weight of her buttock, the heat of her punished flesh against his palm. "Gymnast? Or was it yoga? How'd you get an ass like this, girl?"

Lily made a tiny sound, dropping her head.

He slapped her bottom, a comparatively gentle blow, tightening his grip in her hair.

"Answer me."

"Gymnastics — and — track. Please…"

"Yoga too? Tell me."

He pictured the lithe lines of her body in the early morning light, her outstretched limbs, those supple curves covered in a light sheen of sweat as she moved.

"Yes."

"I knew it. Whatever it is, it's working. This body…*goddamn*. Unbelievable." Lake looked down, lifting each of her plump buttocks in turn upon his palm. "Keep them relaxed, totally relaxed. That's it. I want to watch them move."

He let each one drop then bounced them on his hand, slapping them back and forth, loving how they wobbled and shuddered, the soft, silky weight of them making him want to sink a gentle bite into her flesh, glorying in her quiet acquiescence to his fondling of her body.

"Good marks here. I'll be leaving more soon."

"Please, Lake. No…"

"Shh, Lily." His fingers delved between her legs, finding the slick evidence that gave lie to her words. "This says what your words don't. You may not have liked your punishment, but your pussy is dripping. Part of you liked it. A lot." He patted those plump, soft labia he already wanted to taste again. "Don't worry though. You'll be getting more of what you need."

With a confusing mix of pride and guilt, he stroked the darkening bruise across her thigh, and she hissed, her body tensing.

"Just checking it, girl. It's okay." He caressed her thighs, rubbing the swollen marks there gently. "I may have something for these. Later though."

His hands explored every inch of her skin, testing the pliability of her flesh with a pinch here, a little slap there, squeezing the smooth muscles, fingertips coursing down the bumps of her spine. Her form trembled, the tension within her vibrating off her body.

She's afraid of you, Lake.

In another time, that realization might have horrified him, made him recoil. But he knew that was far from all she was feeling, and the very fact that those contradictory feelings so obviously warred within her, only fed his lust more, the perverse thrill at playing her own body off against her mind filling him with a possessive joy, and a *territoriality* about her body, a body he was increasingly seeing as his to do with however he wished.

He reached up for her hands, closed his fingers around hers as she gripped the ring. Pressing his body to hers, he let her feel the aching hardness of his erection against her. She shuddered with a long shaky exhalation of breath. He savored the scent of her as he kissed her hair, nuzzling those curls at the top of her head. Her body seemed even smaller, more vulnerable, as his big frame crowded her against the wall.

"What are you going...to do?"

"What do you want me to do, Lily?"

He felt the slightest of movements of her hips against him.

"You were going to"—she swallowed—"use that. Weren't you?"

"Use what? I want to hear you say it." His hand smoothed down the unruly curls of her hair, moving the weight of it to one side to bare the expanse of her smooth skin, to feel the taut muscles of her back.

"Your cock." Her voice grew stronger. "You want to

fuck me."

He looked down, smiling. "To be honest, I was thinking of whipping this plump little bottom of yours again. And thinking about that makes my cock hard, Lily."

"Why? I did...what you told me to do."

Another small, but definite, movement of her hips against him.

"There doesn't need to be a reason, girl." A shudder passed through her body, and he pressed himself to her harder, his lips moving against the wisps of her hair. "That bothers you, doesn't it? That I'd punish you just because I wanted to? Or does it confuse you? Do you wonder why your cunt is dripping at the idea?"

"I'll never want you, Lake. Never."

"If I reach down to feel that pussy of yours, I'm going to find it soaking wet, aren't I? What do you think that says? I think it terrifies you to know your body wants what it wants." His finger tapped the back of her skull. "No matter what the mind says."

"Chemistry isn't love. It means...nothing."

"Doesn't it?" He grasped a fistful of her hair, wrenching her head back, making her hiss with the pain. He tasted her trembling lips, felt the heat of her rapid breaths, as he kissed her harder. He explored her mouth possessively. That mouth, those soft, swollen lips were his, just as the rest of her was. He pressed quick soft kisses to the corners of her mouth, the tip of her nose, even a long, gentle one over her moist eye. He'd tried to fight this before, the passion rising within him, and barely succeeded, but now he gave in to it, kissing her savagely again, her lost moan swallowed up by his ravenous lips. Her tongue met his, tentatively at first, then she gave way, kissing him back, surrendering to his control, to his lust.

Running his hand down her body, he plunged it between her cheeks, seeking the wet heat of her sex. He could already smell her on the air in the small, still room, the scent of her arousal unmistakable, something he knew he'd never tire of. His fingers slipped between those bare, swollen lips, plunging deep, testing her, confirming what her words denied.

"So wet," he breathed against her lips, pressing a hard kiss to her once more, triumphant, catching her lip between his teeth, making her whine even as her bottom pressed urgently against him now.

"No," she said. "I don't…"

"Don't fight it, Lily. It doesn't matter anymore. Just let go." His fingertips slid over her hard clit, circling it gently then more insistently at her hard gasp, her thighs squeezing his hand. "There's no right or wrong in this. Let go."

"Lake…I can't. Please."

"You can, Lily." He brought his sopping fingers up to her lips, forcing them into her mouth for her to suck. He pulled them away, kissing her again, tasting her upon her lips, his mouth watering at the clean scent of her. "This says it. This is the real you. Stop fighting it. Stop pretending and be who you really are."

"I don't know…who that is anymore." She jerked up onto her toes, panting as his fingers worked her clit even harder, the little bundle of nerves growing bigger by the second. "I don't…"

"You do know, Lily." He leaned his forehead against her temple, his lips caressing the curve of her ear. "You're *mine*. Accept it."

He curled his fingers into her cunt, the shocking wetness making him growl with animal lust. She reared up, groaning as he alternated stroking within her heated sex and worrying the hard bud of her clit.

"Let go, Lily. Give me this. Surrender to it."

He worked at her cunt harder, the curling strokes of his fingers coming faster and faster, her hips bucking up and down as his hand thrust into her.

"Lake! Ah God, that's…oh *fuck*!"

He smiled at the urgent need he heard in her voice, her

swollen pink lips locked in an O, her eyes squeezed shut, that gorgeous hair wild around her blushing cheeks.

"Please! Oh God, please!"

"Let go," he said against her ear. "Just let go, Lily girl."

One last, hard curl of his fingers within her and she let go a harsh, almost surprised scream, her body convulsing, her head thrown back against his shoulder, teeth clenched. He made her ride his fingers all through those gushing convulsions, her juices bathing his hand and wrist, dripping to the floorboards between her feet.

"Oh my God! Oh my God!"

"Yes, let it come, girl. Let it come. I want all of it."

He swirled a fingertip over the hard, swollen clit, and she screamed louder, her entire body stiffening, her hips rotating against his painful erection in a halting, bucking rhythm.

Lake kept at her, the wet sounds if his fingers plundering her cunt, not letting her rest, the dripping, molten sex widening around not one but three fingers now as he forced them deep, pushing her up onto her toes once more, her head, the dark curls sodden with sweat, falling forward between her outstretched arms.

"No…God, I can't…again."

"Yes, you can, girl. You'll come for me again."

Twice more, his relentless fingers stirred her up again, mercilessly working the hard and no doubt sore little clit until he brought her to climax, and twice more, she screamed out her release, her voice growing ragged as she pleaded though her final orgasm, sweat running down the sweet trough of her spine, her entire body trembling, legs shaking as he let her back down to her feet with a gentle, wet slap of his hand against her soft buttocks. She let go of the ring, sagging to her knees, leaning against the wall as he let her go, tears streaming down her face, words tumbling from her lips, almost unintelligible.

"No…more, so…much. God, Lake…"

But he wasn't done.

He dropped to one knee behind her, one hand working at his fly, the other catching up her hands in his, pulling her to her feet with ridiculous ease, marveling again at how small she was, how light she felt in his hands.

"Put those arms against the wall, girl. Move your feet back."

His throat felt constricted, the effort to form words becoming more difficult as he looked down at the blushing, bruised buttocks, jiggling as she haltingly obeyed.

"Lake..."

"Farther, Lily. Stick that bottom out now."

She looked back at him, her eyes glazed over.

"Face forward," he barked, giving her ass a harsh slap. "And keep that head down."

Her curls flew as she obeyed instantly, dropping her head between her arms, her fingers working against the rough surface of the wall above her, her forearms braced against the wood.

He had to crouch down some, the differences in their heights stark in this position, his hand clamped to her hip, steadying her swaying bottom. His cock jutted before him, bouncing as he adjusted position. He slapped it against her soft buttocks, taking firm hold of her sore cheeks and yawning them apart, exposing her cleft to his gaze. He touched the broad, weeping head of his cock to her tight little bottom hole, smiling as it tightened further in fear. He wiped the pre-come onto the silky smooth, vulnerable flesh of her anus, her breath coming in harsh gusts.

"Please. Not there, Lake," she said, desperation, and something else, in her tone. Her voice had gone husky, almost rough, from her screaming, and he found he liked the sound of it very much.

He swirled a thumb over her cringing bottom hole, spreading the liquid over it until it shone with slickness, then he tapped the broad head of his cock against the wet, vulnerable anus. "Relax, Lily girl. I'm not taking this ass — yet. Just something for you to think about for the future."

He placed his cock against the slickened labia, luxuriating in the feeling of anticipation, noting the way Lily's thighs tensed, but her hips canted back subtly, opening herself ever so slightly, her body betraying her yet again. He thumbed the soft, wet labia wide, the vision of the bright pink of her inner flesh making his mouth go dry, the slickened lips of her sex catching the light.

No going back from here, Lake.

He stood at the Rubicon now. This really was it, and no amount of rationalization or equivocation would change the truth of things. But as he looked down upon her, caressing the round bottom spread before him, the scent of her cunt making his mouth water, he knew what would be done. Right or wrong, there was no longer any doubt.

"Try to relax, girl. Stay still. Very quiet now."

He slid into her in one long, firm stroke, forcing a yelp from her lips as he made her take the full length of him. She shuddered, and he threw his head back, his eyes closing at the feel of her pussy clamping him in that heated embrace, one he knew he'd never tire of. He sighed, letting her buttocks close once more, transferring his grip to her slim waist, using it to pull her tight to him as he took up slow, deep thrusts, reveling in the whimpers and gasps he wrung from her as his cock plundered her depths. She surprised him. She was a slight woman, and he was a big man, yet she took every inch, even as it made her pant and groan on every deep thrust.

"Lake, oh fuck…"

"Tell me, Lily. Tell me."

He gave her harder, more punishing thrusts, her curls bouncing as she braced against the wall.

"Feels…so good." Her voice broke on the last word, and she shook her head as if to fight the words themselves. "God, so…good."

He took her even harder then, his need to be inside her overtaking all sense or reason. He was embarrassingly close to coming already, but he couldn't stop. There'd have to be another time for relishing the clench and squeeze of her soft pussy as he fucked her. Now there was only his blind animal lust. She cried out as he rammed into her even harder, the head of his cock striking her cervix.

She moaned, reaching down between the wall and her body, pinching her own nipple.

"More. Oh fuck...more!"

Reaching under her, he closed a hand over hers, making her pinch harder, slapping her bouncing breasts then helping her squeeze those nipples again until she whimpered with the pain.

He smacked her ass, hard, taking a handful of her hair and pulling on it as he brought her completely off her feet, staked upon his cock. He crushed her against the wall, her cheek against the wood, her moans rising with each ever-harder drive into her depths.

"Fuck! So hard...so hard!"

"That's right, slut," he ground out, pinning her to the wall, his hips pistoning against her, driving the breath from her. "Almost there. Fuck, your cunt...so tight."

He looked down, loving the way his thick shaft spread her little pussy wide as he pushed as deep as he could, the feel of his pubic hair rasping against her hot, soft buttocks, the slap of his flesh against her. Her juices were so copious, he could feel them dripping from his swinging balls.

Reluctant she may have been, but her body had completely surrendered to lust.

"I'm going to..." She grew more frantic in her movements, her hand clamping onto his forearm the nails digging into his flesh with a flash of hot pain. "Coming...Lake"

His hand slipped down and found her sensitive clit again. If anything, it was even harder, more prominent than it had been before. As his fingertips stroked around it, then over it in quick circles, she cried out, her nails digging into his forearm even deeper.

"Oh God. Hurts, Lake! Too much!"

"This little clit's sensitive, isn't it?" He gave it a tweak, and she let out a lost shriek. "You're going to come one more time, slut. Once more. I'm not done fucking you until you come."

And come she did, as his fingers worked that clit mercilessly, as she pleaded with him to stop, to never stop, that she was going to die. Then she exploded, thrashing between him and the wall, her writhing hips bouncing him away before he caught his balance, pinning her again as he whispered promises and threats in her ear. He gently squeezed her mons in his palm as he brought her down, his cock pounding away within the tight, wet clutch of her cunt the entire time. He brought them down to their knees, then, and he pressed her head to the floor, her hands at the base of the wall.

He stroked her sweat-soaked hair as he switched to slow, steady thrusts, his cock now screaming for a release that he was just barely able to stave off.

"Very still," he said in a low, strained voice. "Very quiet now, Lily. I'm gonna fuck this cunt now."

He plunged then as far as he could, slowly, slowly until she'd taken all of him again, and she moaned at the incredibly tight fit, her buttocks twitching under the grip of his palms. Holding himself still inside her, he reveled anew at the way she writhed beneath him, her head turning left then right, her moans almost continuous.

Incredibly, her cunt squeezed him then, hard, and it set off the chain reaction of his climax. He slammed into her over and over, each thrust driving a cry from her, his hands clamped onto her hips bruisingly hard. Then his orgasm boiled up from behind his testicles, his eyes rolling back as incredible sensation blanked out every sense in the white explosion of pleasure. His come poured forth, filling her to overflowing as the last spurts subsided. He braced himself on his hands over her, his sweat dripping from his chin onto her upper back. She stayed crouched as she was, her bottom high, as he breathed above her like a great bellows.

"Lake...I-I don't..."

"Shh, now. Just relax, girl."

He stroked her hair again and patted her bottom, his cock still deep within her, and only now starting to soften. Her pussy still gave his cock little spasmodic squeezes that made him groan, his teeth clenched. He tightened a hand in her hair, pulling her up until she lay back against his chest, his cock not yet released from the jealous clutch of her wet cunt. He clamped an arm under her breasts and drew her up with him as he stood, the little woman as light as a doll in his arms. She hissed under the stricture of his fist in her hair, and he let it go, the long, sodden curls swinging around her head as it lolled forward, Lily muttering a curse under her breath.

Then he laid her down upon the mattress, pulling her tight to him, his wet cock nestled in the cleft of her bottom, his hand taking firm hold of her breast as he settled her back against his chest.

She murmured something, and he squeezed her closer, giving her soft breast a little slap.

"Sleep, Lily."

CHAPTER 10

The blanket was tucked up under my chin when I woke some time later. The room was dark but for the light that streamed in from the one small window. The memory of what had passed between Lake and I projected its image onto my mind. I closed my eyes against it but it was quickly replaced by another and then another. What had I done? Had I even tried to make him stop? And if I had said no, *would* he have stopped?

The room smelled of sex, of him and of me. My entire body ached, my pussy was sore and when I sat up, the pain on my bottom reminded me of what would happen when I disobeyed.

I pushed the blanket off altogether. Even though it was cold in the room, I didn't want it on me. I wanted a shower and I wanted not to think about what had just happened. This didn't make any sense. The things I was feeling didn't make any sense.

Shivering, I switched on the lamp beside the bed and really took in my surroundings for the first time. The room wasn't very large and looked like a work/guest room. Maybe it had been intended as the former and he'd converted it into the latter when he had decided to kidnap me. But when had he decided to kidnap me?

But did it matter anymore? I was here now.

I tried the door first, knowing it would be locked, and it was. The high window was too small for me to fit through, but at least I could see out if I stood on tiptoe. It must have been early because a low mist covered the ground, the droplets making the grass sparkle in the sun. All I could see—for as far as I could see—were trees. It was beautiful and very different from the city I was used to waking up in. The only sound here was that of birds and nothing else; even the air seemed more still.

News flash, Lily: you're not on a fucking vacation.

Shaking my head, I turned back around to find that the floor in the farthest corner was tiled. It looked like he had been building a bathroom but had stopped partway through. I went on to the boxes stacked against a corner and opened the one on top to find it full of books. I lifted it off and looked inside the next one. Same thing, more books, and the last one was the same. I dusted off my hands and stood then decided to restack the boxes so he wouldn't know I'd looked inside them. Part of me rebelled against that last little act, not liking the fact that it was a sign of my fear of him, of what he could and would do to me, but I pushed it aside and continued my search.

The closet was next. There was no lock on the door and I opened it to find snowshoes and two pair of cross-country skis. I even picked up one of the poles but put it back down. What was I going to do, swing it at him? Then what? Get punished again, that's what. If I was going to physically attack Lake, I'd have to make sure I killed him this time. Or at least knocked him out long enough to get out before he could grab me. I would never be able to overpower him otherwise.

A suitcase was stored on the top shelf and I pulled it

down, sneezing with the dust it brought with it. It was heavier than I'd expected and landed with a thud on the bare floor. Laying it on its side, I unzipped it and pushed back the top then sank back to sit on my heels, goose bumps raising every hair on my body.

Neatly folded clothing and several pairs of shoes filled the case. From the smell of it, it hadn't been opened in a very long time. I lifted out a sweater from the top. It was soft, angora, the color a pretty blush making me think of ashes of roses. I set it aside and picked up another. This one still had a tag on it. It was brand new and in my size. Digging deeper, I found pants, jeans and skirts, several nighties and more sweaters. All of them were the same size, and the shoes were close enough to my own size that I could wear them. I wondered how long he'd had these things, if he'd kidnapped others before me. A new urgency would have sent me into a panic but I heard the key slip into the lock, and, as quickly as I could, I shoved the suitcase back into the closet and closed the door, running to sit on the bed, hoping he wouldn't find out what I'd been doing.

The door opened and I pulled the blanket up to cover myself. When Lake's eyes found mine, heat flooded my face, my cheeks burning at the memory of what had happened between us. But that wasn't all. My body reacted, too, and I became very aware of how my sex seemed to come to attention at his entrance. I dropped my gaze and tugged the blanket closer when he closed the door, only looking up when I heard him locking it again. He carried a mug and the scent of freshly brewed coffee made my mouth water.

"Good morning, princess," he said.

"Is it a good morning? I wouldn't know. I'm locked up in this dusty old shed."

Lake's eyes narrowed but he grinned and took a step closer. "There's my girl," he said. "Slow learner and stubborn as hell, but I wouldn't have it any other way."

I looked away.

"Coffee?" he asked, coming to stand before me.

The mug was steaming and my mouth watered. I nodded, reaching up.

"Ask nicely," he said, holding it just out of reach.

I met his gaze and it took all I had not to think about what he'd done to me, how he'd felt inside me, how many times he'd made me come. "May I have some coffee, please?" I asked, remembering the opened suitcase in the closet, thinking how he'd punish me if he found it, wondering at the clothes there, wondering if there had been others before me, considering what he was capable of doing.

He held the mug out to me and I took it, our fingers touching when I did, my mind recalling where those fingers had been hours before. "Just drink it, no shenanigans," he said, his tone serious, his gaze moving to the strap hanging on the wall.

I nodded but had no intention of throwing it at him if that's what he thought. And I had already seen the strap and had no interest in having another session with it. I brought the mug to my lips but hesitated, looking at him. "You take a sip first," I said.

He laughed but took the mug, sat down next to me and drank. "I have no need to drug you," he said.

He hadn't added any sugar or cream and the taste was bitter. I drank it anyway and the room remained silent until I was finished and handed the mug back to him.

"What now?" I asked, looking at him. My body felt like tiny needles were pricking it all over with him sitting so close.

"I was thinking you'd want a shower and breakfast," he said.

"How long do I have to stay here? I mean..." *Why did you kidnap me?*

"After your shower, you'll come back to the bad girl's room, and you'll stay until I'm satisfied you've learned your lesson. How long will depend on you."

"That's not what I meant and you know it. What happened to the US Marshal?" I finally asked the question.

"Ah," he said. "DeSalvo. Randall paid him to deliver you to him."

I processed this slowly while Lake continued.

"He's probably out looking for you now," Lake continued. "In fact, I'm sure there are a whole army of men out looking for both of us."

"I don't understand. Did my dad hire you or was that a lie?"

"Your dad hired me. So did Randall."

"So why am I here and not there? You'd have to be stupid to double cross them both."

Lake rubbed his face and stood. He inhaled a deep breath and looked at me, then exhaled. "Get up, Lily. If you want that shower that is."

"What, did you kidnap me to *save* me from them? From DeSalvo? Randall?" I paused. "Or were you looking for more money?" He didn't answer, and my gaze moved lower. "And while you were at it, thought you'd get your rocks off?" I snorted, eyes narrowed, ready for a battle, at least a verbal one.

In the silence that followed, I questioned how wise it was to provoke this man.

"Lily girl, you can't help yourself, can you?" he said, shaking his head and walking to the door. "Try to imagine where you might be if it weren't for me. Think what would have happened to you in the custody of the man your father can put away for life. Can you visualize the type of welcome you'd have received there?" he said. "They'd make yesterday's strapping look like a fucking walk in the park." He shook his head and walked toward the door.

"You can't keep me here!" I called out, running after him, one hand clutching the blanket to me as I grabbed his arm.

He turned, grabbing mine hard. "You screwed up your

chance to have a shower." Too fast for me to react, he tore the blanket from me and held me there, naked. His eyes raked over my body before returning to meet my gaze. "You don't listen very well," he said, slapping my hip hard. "What are the rules, Lily?" he asked, smacking again as he walked me back to the bed. "Tell me the rules," he said, easily grabbing hold of my other arm when I swung at him, all the while dragging me toward the bed. "Rules," he repeated, holding both of my wrists at my back in one hand, placing one booted foot on the frame of the bed and leaning me over his thigh, smacking my bottom hard as he spoke. "I asked you for the rules. Do you want to recite them while I spank you with my hand or do you prefer the strap?"

"I hate you!" I yelled, trying to get free or at least to avoid the volley of spanks. He struck the same spot over and over again, making my bottom burn in a very short amount of time especially as it was still sore after yesterday's strapping.

"I guess you want the strap then," he said, reaching for it.

"No, no strap! I'm not to cover myself and I'm only to speak when you ask me a question. I'm sorry, please don't punish me!" I begged, looking back at him over my shoulder.

"Please don't punish me, what?" he asked through clenched teeth.

"Sir. Please don't punish me, Sir."

He dropped me on the bed then and I caught myself before reaching to cover my breasts and set my arms at my sides instead.

He stood looking at me for a minute before replacing the strap on its hook along the wall. Without another word, he turned and walked away, picking up the discarded mug as well as the blanket, and walked out the door, locking it behind him.

"Fuck!"

Captive, Mine

My stomach growled, and I stood. I'd screwed up a chance at a shower and food and instead managed to piss him off. Again.

* * *

He left me alone for what I assumed were a few hours. In that time, I repacked the suitcase as best as I could and put it back where I'd found it.

I went to the dresser I'd not been able to look at earlier and opened the first drawer to find it full of wires and other accessories for various electronics, I assumed. The second one held two thick binders. I opened one and looked through some of the pages. Just random paperwork. I moved on to the last drawer to find picture frames wrapped neatly in packing paper. I unwrapped one but set it aside; it was a boring, standard print, something you'd find at the Ikea. The next two were the same. It was when I got to the fourth one that I was surprised. It was the only personal photograph in the drawer. I looked at it closely, almost not recognizing the man who now held me captive. I stood and walked to the bed, studying it as I sat on the edge of the bed. It was a photo taken in the summertime in San Francisco. I recognized the place, a popular tourist spot along the Wharf. Lake looked relaxed and happy. He was laughing, and he had his arm around a woman. She was staring up at him, and she, too, was laughing. I looked more closely. She was pretty, with light brown hair and blue eyes. She had her hand on his chest and was leaning into him, into his embrace. Lake's hand was wrapped around her waist possessively, and there, on one finger, shone a band of gold.

Was he married, or had he been once? He looked younger in the photo, but that could have been because he was smiling too. It's not like I saw him doing that very often. Regardless, I didn't care about Lake's personal life. I couldn't imagine he was married anymore, even if he had been once. He didn't wear a wedding band now, and he certainly couldn't have time to keep a wife *and* kidnap me. I got up to put the photo away, but when I did, I managed to drop the damn thing. I quickly picked it up, noticing how the glass had cracked right between the happy couple.

I touched the spot then put the photograph away and closed the drawer, hoping he wouldn't find it.

It was when I was standing on one of the boxes I'd moved beneath the window to look outside that I heard the door again. I panicked for a moment but it was too late to put the box away, so I stood there instead, my back to the wall as he came inside carrying a bucket, a towel under his arm, and two water bottles. When he saw me, he raised an eyebrow. "Redecorating?" he asked, setting the bucket down. It splashed sudsy water onto the floor when he did. He then locked the door before turning to me.

I, meanwhile, kept my hands at my sides, remembering the rules. This next part was going to kill me, but I took a deep breath and forced myself to speak. "Sir?" I asked, trying hard to keep the sarcasm from my voice.

His face told me how surprised he was at my tone. He nodded, which I assumed meant for me to go on.

"I'm sorry about earlier. It's only that...I don't understand."

He looked at me. "Come here," he said.

I hesitated briefly, glancing at the strap on the wall, but walked to him. He held out one of the water bottles, and I took it.

"It's a protein shake. Drink it."

I sniffed the bottle — fake chocolate. "I don't like protein sh—" I began but the look on his face told me to stop talking, and I did. He waited and watched while I drank the gritty shake down. When it was finished, I wiped my mouth off and handed the empty bottle back to him.

"This is not a fucking resort, in case you hadn't noticed," he said, taking it back. "Drinking water is there." He pointed to the other bottle. "And this," he began, hauling the bucket to where the bathroom would have been. "Is your bath." He reached into the bucket and picked up the sponge, holding it out to me. "I'll be back to inspect you in ten minutes."

"Inspect me?"

"Yes. I've decided we'll make it a regular thing. It will be good for you, I think. For your pride. Ten minutes. Be a good girl, Lily," he said as he unlocked the door.

This wasn't anything I was expecting. "How long will you keep me here? What you said earlier…"

"Nine minutes," he said and walked out the door.

I hated the sound of that door locking. Rubbing my forehead, I went to the unfinished bathroom and picked up the sponge. The water was only lukewarm, but I washed myself, not sure when I would get a proper shower or even another bucket of water. I needed to wash my hair too, but that wasn't going to work.

Part of me wanted to pretend I didn't understand what he meant by an inspection, but I knew full well. He would humiliate me again, rape me again.

Rape. Could what had happened be called rape? How many times had I come? How many times had I tried to fight? Too many on the former and not even once on the latter. But I was afraid and I hadn't known what he would do. How far he would go. I wondered if he knew it himself.

After scrubbing myself clean, I dumped the sponge back into the bucket and picked up the towel to dry off. I was not about to give that final thought a moment of attention. Lake Freeman knew exactly what he was doing. He had probably been planning on kidnapping me all along.

As for DeSalvo and Randall and saving me from them? I shook my head, thinking. It didn't make sense. As long as Lake kept me, he'd be a wanted man. And a dead one if either the US Marshal or Randall caught up with him. So why keep me? He wasn't a bad-looking guy and if he were, he could pay any whore for sex. This wasn't about sex.

Money? I shook my head again as the lock turned and Lake walked in. I looked at him, holding tight to the towel. This wasn't about money either.

Maybe I just like to keep pretty girls chained to my bed. Why didn't the memory of those words repel me?

He locked the door. I remained standing where I was without saying a word, waiting. My sex tightened as I looked back at him, knowing what he expected. I was in the bad girl's room. I'd have to be a good girl to leave it.

Holding his gaze, I unwrapped the towel, dropped it to the floor, and stood before him naked with my arms at my sides, waiting for my inspection.

Lake's gaze traveled up and down my body, causing a shiver to run along my spine. "Good girl," he said. "You're learning. Up against the wall facing me now, hands on top of your head, legs shoulder width."

My belly quivered, and although it wasn't resistance I felt, neither was it a desire to please. I wanted him to make me. It would be easier if he made me.

No words came while we stood there and I hoped he could read not defiance but an inability to speak or move in my eyes.

"Up against the wall, Lily."

I tried to open my mouth but couldn't. Instead, I pulled my arms tighter to my sides, my shoulders rounding a little. That prickling feeling was back and it was all over. I stood there staring at him, watching his expression change as I shook my head no.

"That's not how good girls behave," he said calmly. "Shame." He walked over to me and somehow, I didn't move away. His eyes weren't angry, not like they had been when I'd tried to stab him with those ridiculous clippers. They looked as though he wasn't entirely surprised by my non-action.

"You're not shy all of a sudden, are you?" he asked, gripping me by the back of my neck. "I've seen and touched every inch of you and, if I recall," he continued, walking me toward the bed, "you liked it," he said. He looked at me with a wicked grin on his face, his hand squeezing hard.

"You're hurting me," I managed, still not fighting but

not quite compliant either.

"Get the strap and hand it to me," he said.

I tried to pull away at that but when I did, he shifted his grip to take a fistful of my hair instead.

"Ow!" I clamped my hand around his wrist, trying to pull him off.

"And then get on your hands and knees on the bed. Ass to me, your face buried in the mattress."

"No."

He carried on as if I'd not said a word. "If I have to get it myself and hold you down to punish you, you'll take twenty strokes, but if you can show me you can obey, it'll only be ten," he said, shaking me once, forcing me to look at him. "What will it be?"

"I'm sorry. Please, I don't want that strap..."

He tugged again.

"I'll do what you say. I'll stand at the wall like you said."

"You keep missing the opportunities I give you, Lily. First the shower and a decent breakfast, and now a simple order to stand at the wall for inspection. Am I holding you down or are you bending over and offering your ass for your strokes?" he asked. "That's the choice we're working with now. I'll count to three, and if you haven't decided, I'll assume you want the twenty. One."

"Wait. No."

"Two."

"Lake..."

He opened his mouth.

"Ten! I want ten! Please!"

"Please, what?"

"Please, Sir!"

He released me instantly and gestured to the strap. Tears of panic filled my eyes. This wasn't how this was supposed to go. I squeezed my eyes shut and forced a deep breath in before opening them again. "Please Lake, I'm sorry. Can we just start again? Please?"

"Strap, Lily."

I was already crying by the time I took the strap from the wall. The leather felt strange in my trembling hands, thick and flexible, frightening. I handed it to him, wanting to get rid of it. He took it and gestured to the bed. My tears came faster, but I obeyed. I was getting strapped; that was a certainty. All I had control over was whether I was getting ten or twenty strokes.

I knelt on the bed with my back to him, wiped my face, and planted my hands, waiting.

"Almost there. Get down on your elbows and get your face down on the bed. Ass up in the air and don't move."

I did it, somehow, moved into the position he wanted me in. The palm of his hand came to my low back and pressed so my hips lifted higher.

"Just like that," he said, stepping back. Then, a few moments later, while I waited, unable to breathe, to blink, to think, "I like your ass, Lily."

I gasped when he struck.

"I like looking at it, and I like punishing it." Another lash had me crying out and breaking position so he had to wait until I was once again ready to take the next stroke.

"I'm going to like fucking it, too." Another stroke. "And I most definitely"—two more stripes burned into me—"prefer it striped red to pristine white."

He didn't speak after that but laid each stroke with hardly a break between them, concentrating on my sit spots. Ten strokes that felt like a hundred and I wasn't sure how I had taken the punishment of the previous night. Or was it the previous day? I didn't even know anymore.

When the ten were over, I remained in position on the bed, shaking. Lake hung the strap up and came back to me, sitting down on the bed and petting my hair.

"Shh, it's over now. You think you can get into position for that inspection now?" he asked almost kindly, even though we both knew he wasn't asking at all.

I wiped my face and nodded even while I still cried.

The skin of my ass felt tight and hot and he had to help me off the bed, my legs were shaking so badly. I managed to move though, managed to get to the wall where he stood me. Managed to get my hands on top of my head and my legs spread to shoulder width, sniffling while Lake looked me over.

"You could have avoided all of that, you know," he said, taking a tissue and wiping my eyes and nose while I nodded. "Remember it the next time you're told to do something, Lily."

I sucked in a shaky breath and nodded again, lowering my gaze, but he took hold of my chin gently and lifted my face to look up at him.

"What do you say, Lily?" he asked.

"Yes, Sir. I'm sorry, Sir."

He smiled and some part of me felt almost proud at that. "Good girl. Now let's have a look at you."

He stepped back a little and my inspection began.

He didn't speak so much as mutter sounds of approval as he lifted each of my breasts, slapping them softly. He squeezed one hardened nipple, making me cry out, making it difficult to keep my hands where they were. He then trailed his fingertips over my belly and down to my sex. He leaned down and pressed his thumb against the stubble there. I was normally waxed bare but it had been a few weeks. He clucked his tongue and looked at me. "We'll have to take care of this," he said. "Don't want you looking sloppy." He straightened then and patted my hip. "You know how this is going to go, right? Turn around, take your legs wider and bend over. Hands around your ankles."

Why this still made me flush with embarrassment I wasn't sure. The expression in his eyes was hard, inflexible, and I knew I had no choice. I had to get through this. Why did it matter anyway? He was right. He'd seen every inch of me. He'd fucked me. Why was this so damn hard?

I turned and widened my stance. He stepped back and

audibly sucked in a breath as I bent and took hold of my ankles.

"You'll want to avoid more spanking for the next few days at least," he said, making me wince when he touched my welted bottom. He then spread my cheeks wide. "What's this, Lily?" he asked, two fingers running over the folds of my sex. "You're wet."

I sucked in that breath when his hands slid forward and two fingers found my swollen clit.

"Do you like doing as you're told?" he asked, rubbing harder, making me take one hand to the floor to support myself. "I'll have to check you more closely next time I spank you," he continued. "Maybe it's the pain that gets you wet."

"No," I managed.

"No, I shouldn't check you more closely or no, you don't like the pain because something's got you soaking here, girl?" As he said it, his other hand pulled my cheeks wider and a finger dipped into my pussy once, twice, before trailing the cleft up to my bottom hole and the pad of that finger, wet with my own arousal, began to circle my anus. "And this?" he asked, working my clit harder. When he pressed his finger into the tight hole, I sucked in a breath, all of my muscles tightening. "How tight is this hole?" he said more to himself than to me. "Has it ever been fucked?"

I groaned, clenching against him as he pushed in to one knuckle. It hurt a little but it was more the embarrassment than anything else.

The fingers working my clit were gone and I felt a light slap to my hip.

"When I ask you a question, you answer it," he said, thrusting his finger into my ass, making me call out with the sudden pain of the rough intrusion. "I'm feeling generous so I'll repeat myself. Have you ever been fucked in the ass, Lily?"

"No!"

"No, what?" he asked, pulling out and pushing in again, slowly this time.

"No, Sir." I said, my reward his fingers returning to my clit. I hated this, hated wanting how it felt, hated him for making me want it.

"So you've never come with a cock in your ass?" he taunted, still slowly moving inside me, pulling all the way out then pushing back in. The sensation was so different from anything I'd felt before, so much more intense.

"No, Sir," I said through a shudder.

"You're tight, Lily, girl," he said, "I'll have to ready you to take my cock here."

"No, no, no..." I began, rising a little, hating myself for not trying harder to pull away.

"Shh," he coaxed, his hand at my back, his fingers wet on my skin. "Back down now, girl. I'm not going to fuck your ass today. Hands back around your ankles."

I mewled but resumed my position and he resumed the rubbing of my clit, pinching it harder now as he added a second finger into my asshole.

I was barely able to hold still and to my shame, couldn't remain quiet as he brought me to the very edge of orgasm.

"Not today. Today you'll come with my fingers in your ass and you'll learn how good girls, girls who do as they're told, are rewarded," he said. "Come, Lily."

CHAPTER 11

His phone finally rang while he was on his walk out to the shed. The day was overcast, but still reasonably warm — perfect for what he had in mind. He'd seen the boxes under the window when he'd gone in to see Lily, the way she'd stood there, guilty, caught with her hand in the cookie jar. Lily had been a bad girl, so he needed to take care of that little problem.

Lake put the phone to his ear as he sorted through the mess of the shed. "Tell me you got the car."

"I could tell you that, but it wouldn't be true."

Lake sighed, but inside he was relieved. For every day that elapsed since his last call with his fixer, he doubted more and more he'd ever hear from him again.

"So, what happened? You found it, didn't you?"

"Yep. But someone else found it first." Kellen paused a moment. "I parked the truck about half a click past the quarry and walked down to it. Never got close to the car though. Place was crawling."

"Cops?"

Lake's heartbeat began to thud. This was...not good.

"No way. Two vans, no markings. Suits. One tall motherfucker seemed to be running the show."

"Dark hair?"

"Affirmative."

DeSalvo.

A rake fell against the steel wall of the shed, the sound ringing in Lake's ears. "Jesus."

"I got good eyes on 'em through the scope—"

"You had your weapon on them?"

"Had no idea who they were. Of course I had my weapon on 'em. Had a good field of fire from a thick stand along a ridgeline to the northeast, just in case. Was a fucking bitch to get up there though."

No cops.

He agreed with Kellen — definitely no cops, yet. Had DeSalvo informed the US Marshals though? That wasn't clear. The men described could easily be more marshals or Randall's men. He'd have to assume DeSalvo wasn't the only corrupt marshal, so at this point it didn't matter. The good news was, no cops. At worst, DeSalvo was trying to at least keep the news within the Marshals Service. But if Lake were in DeSalvo's shoes? No way would he let the Marshals Service know he'd lost custody of Lily. It had to be Randall's men then. It would give them more time.

But they had the car now.

"Kellen, were you followed?"

"No way. I watched them all go then humped it through the bush back to my truck. No roads on foot."

"You need to get gone. Now."

Lake tried to think. They probably had time, after all. The car complicated things, but without the police involved, they were likely safe. For now. With the car, DeSalvo could keep the cops ignorant as to what had really happened, and he could probably string the Marshals Service along for as long as he needed too. If it was Randall's men searching for them, they'd take their time, be careful.

Eventually though, they'd likely zero in. Nothing obvious connected Lake or Lily to his cabin. But cartels were fiendishly clever — and relentless. He'd done enough business with them over the years to know.

Someday, they'd find them.

"You heard me, right? They had no idea I was there, boss."

"Kellen, listen to me, and do what I tell you." Lake paused to calm his voice. "If they get hold of you, we're all dead. Do you understand me?"

"Affirmative."

"Gone — and stay gone. I don't want to hear from you anytime soon, you got me?"

"You plannin' on telling me what the fuck's going on?"

Lake rubbed a hand across his forehead. "That big mother you got a bead on? Crooked marshal. Randall owns him."

Kellen whistled.

"They were going to take Lily Cross hostage." Lake winced. "And I was going to hand her over to Randall."

Even over the phone, he could feel Kellen cool.

"I should've told you, Kellen, but it was my last job. Shitty thing to do to you, I know. I'm sorry for it."

"Why do you have her now? Why bring an entire cartel and a crooked marshal down on you? Makes no fucking sense, boss."

"DeSalvo...was going to work her over first."

"Fucking prick. I knew I should've fired him up. Had his mug right in the crosshairs..."

"I couldn't let him do it." Lake kicked an old can of spray paint, sending it spinning back into the darkness of a corner of the shed. "Just couldn't."

"Never could resist the rescues, could you?" Kellen gave him his trademark wry chuckle. Lake suddenly feared he'd never hear it again.

"Best thing to do right now is stay out of sight. Out of

country, if you can swing it. I don't know how much they checked into me, but it's a good bet they know you're an associate. They'll assume it. So, get gone."

He finally spotted the can he was looking for. Now, he had to find a damned brush.

"I'm off the grid in one hour, boss. I don't expect I'll be talking to you again, will I?"

"No, I don't expect you will, Kellen."

"Take care of her. But don't be a fucking hero."

No danger of heroism here! Monster.

The line went dead.

Lake looked up at the trees swaying gently in the warm wind. "Good luck, my friend."

He finally found the brush and headed back.

* * *

He didn't even make the second brush stroke down the glass before Lily's pretty face appeared on the other side of the window. Her eyes were wide, the question on her lips. But he simply smiled at her, adding another broad swath of black paint.

This is fucked up, Lake.

"You passed fucked up about six exits ago, dude," Lake muttered.

Lily's lips moved, the sound only barely discernable over the whispering of the breeze through the leaves. "Why?"

She needed to learn. Every time she was defiant, every time she pushed the boundaries, the stricter he'd become, the more of her freedom she'd be relinquishing. Soon, he hoped she'd really understand, and he could go easy on her again.

But now was not that time, unfortunately.

He knew the paint wouldn't block out all the light, but that would be to his advantage. It would let in just enough so that Lily could see what her behavior was depriving her of, the wages of disobedience to him.

As Lake completed the last stroke over the glass, the window fully blacked out, he set down the paint can, laying the brush across the top. For a moment, he closed his eyes, searching his mind, taking stock about what was okay, and what was, well, evil. This wasn't evil, *quite*. Did this need to be done? Yes, she had to learn. Especially when it came time to flee — and that time was coming, the only question was when. He knew it, deep down, no matter how much he wished it weren't so.

Lily had to learn to obey him instantly, instinctively. It was going to be hard for her, but for now, anyway, he had the time to be both patient and relentless. He'd teach her, mold her, make her what he needed her to be — what *she* needed to be, though she'd never admit it.

And, someday, it might just save their lives.

Rationalizer.

He wasn't though, not really. Yes, he enjoyed this, took pleasure in bending her strong will to his. There was no denying that fact, and it was something they both knew now. The only question was how far she could be bent before she broke. He'd take her right up to that point, but not past it. Breaking Lily wasn't what he wanted. That *would* truly be evil.

But they had a lot farther to go before they reached that point. And it made no sense not to acknowledge that he looked forward to it with a dark anticipation that fired his imagination, his possessiveness, and his lust.

He snapped the lid onto the paint can and walked back toward the shed, breathing deeply of the fragrant, clean scent of a forest afternoon. Then he stopped in his tracks, remembering. When he'd last been inside to see her, there'd been that box next to her, the one she'd climbed onto to look out the window. That box hadn't been there before.

She'd moved it.

Lake sighed in resignation, even as his cock hardened at what lay ahead. It was time for the next step with Lily.

CHAPTER 12

My first proper meal in what felt like days consisted of tuna from a can and some saltine crackers — and I'd never tasted anything more delicious. Lake simply watched me while I devoured everything he put in front of me and I didn't care for a second what I looked like as I shoved crackers and chunks of tuna into my mouth.

"How many days have we been here?" I asked after downing a glass of water.

"A few," he answered, always a wealth of information.

I looked at him looking at me as if he were waiting for me to challenge him. Well, I wasn't going to do that. I didn't want to go back to the bad girl's room. I never wanted to go back there again.

"Can I call my dad? Tell him I'm okay?"

Lake shook his head, rubbing his chin with his hand. "Not yet. We can't take a chance on anyone tracing the call."

"If he thinks Randall has me, he won't testify."

"I know. Believe me, I know. The quicker he testifies, the quicker this mess is over."

"Why are you doing this?" I asked, knowing that when he had taken me from DeSalvo, no matter how I wanted to fault him for what he'd done to me since, he had saved my life.

"Finish up," he said, standing.

I forced the last bite, no longer hungry. "I'm cold." I hugged my arms around myself. I wore a T-shirt he had given me, one of his. It was entirely too big, but at least I wasn't naked anymore.

Lake got up and picked up a discarded blanket from the couch. He brought it over and instead of handing it to me, he tucked it in behind my back. I met his gaze as I took the corners of it, suspicious of this little act of kindness.

"Are you finished?" he asked.

"Yes."

"I've got some work to do so you'll go back to your room until I'm done."

"I'd really like to have a shower, Lake. I'll be quick. Please...Sir?"

"Now, that is sweet," he began, tucking my hair behind my ear before pushing my chair back and motioning for me to stand. "But I've got a little work to do. I've got to get some things ready in case we need to get out of here in a hurry. Once I'm done, you can have that shower and you can take as long as you like."

"I won't do anything, I promise."

"Don't whine, Lily," he said, opening my bedroom door. "In you go. When I'm back, you can have that shower first thing. I promise."

"Are you going away?"

"Not far. To the room you recently vacated."

I stepped into my bedroom and turned, puzzled. "What do you have to do there?" If he looked closely at anything I'd touched, he'd know I'd been snooping. But really, did he think I wouldn't? I was his captive, I hadn't forgotten that, and I wouldn't, no matter what happened between us. At that thought, I felt my face heat up and dropped my gaze from his. When I looked up a moment later, I found his gaze still on mine, studying me.

"Why don't you get some sleep while I'm gone? You look tired."

A few days ago, I'd have had a comeback for that, but today, I simply nodded and went to the bed. He closed the door and I heard to the deadbolt slide into place as I climbed beneath the sheets and tucked the blanket he'd given me up to my neck, falling asleep as soon as I closed my eyes.

* * *

Lake stood up from the opened boxes, running a hand through his now sweaty hair.

"Goddammit."

He knew he should've moved those boxes. But every time he'd seen Lily in that room, waiting, fearing, wanting — removing those boxes had taken a backseat to the needs of his cock, his need to conquer the bewitching, maddening captive in his care.

"Care," he grunted. "I'm sure that's *exactly* what she'd call it, Lake."

She'd definitely rifled through the boxes. He'd always packed precisely, and his memory never failed him. She'd been through all of it. Probably frantically shoved it all back in as he turned the key in the lock. He was surprised she'd left the boxes out in the open under that window. Maybe she'd hoped he wouldn't notice — or maybe she'd hoped he would.

Either way, it was a problem. But he had a solution for it. He glanced at the length of leather hanging on the wall. She feared it, which was exactly how he wanted it. She still didn't fear him — at least not completely — but she feared that strap.

Lily's bottom was about to become reacquainted with—

He froze.

Where is it?

It was the last picture of Sara he'd let himself keep. Even though every time he looked at it, the memory still burned, still ached as if he'd found her only yesterday, the needle still in her arm, as incriminating as a murder weapon.

He'd burned all of her pictures, knowing he didn't need them, didn't need the agony of seeing her beautiful form before the drugs had wrought their horrors upon her, before she'd become something he no longer recognized.

She had no fucking *right*.

He opened the drawer again, carefully sorting through

the contents, and finally found it. The picture, still in the frame that had always been its home — but with the wrapping gone and a new crack in the glass. He'd remembered precisely how he'd laid it inside. Out of sight, but never out of mind. Someday he'd hoped he could burn that one too, when the memory of his wife no longer filled him with hurt, and rage, and loss. But that day had not yet come.

Red tinged his vision as he went through everything, sorting the contents of each box, the rage and helplessness filling him as each second ticked by. He flung open the closet, spotting the fresh paths left by slender fingers through the dust that coated the suitcase. He didn't need to unzip the suitcase — he knew she'd been in there too.

He closed the closet, leaning a head against the door a moment then backing away. When the backs of his thighs hit the bed, he dropped to the mattress, holding his head in his hands.

Why had he kept it all? He remembered the sweater he'd bought for Sara just…before. He'd stubbornly bought it in the size she'd been before the wasting, before she'd become the wan, sunken-cheeked wreck the heroin had reduced her to.

"No," he whispered.

He hadn't known. Yet he'd kept all of it. Why? Was it some sort of totem he hoped would lead her spirit back to him? Was it denial? Was it premonition? It didn't matter. What mattered was that Sara was gone, that the scum who trafficked in the shit had taken her from him, deprived him of his one chance at a life. It was done. All of it.

And yet, less than a hundred feet away, was a woman who'd wormed her way into parts of him he thought he'd walled off forever. A woman who was also a part of the grotesque machinery that had chewed Sara up and spit her out. The same woman who'd invaded this last vestige of happy memory, of the life torn away.

The woman who *dared* make him think about…what

might be.
Oh, Lily girl, you're in trouble.

* * *

"**G**et up."

My mind was foggy, the dream slowly fading as someone shook me.

"I said, get up, bad girl."

At those last two words, my eyelids flew open. Lake's big hand shook me again, pulling the blanket from me, and the moment I saw his face, his eyes, I knew he knew. I knew he'd seen what I'd done.

"I could have kept you bound," he began, hauling me to my feet.

"Lake, stop…"

"But I was being nice."

"Nice? Nice by keeping me locked up? What are you doing?" Panic rose in my voice as he dragged me by the arm to the door. "No!" I grabbed hold of the doorframe. "No! I'm not going back to that room."

I knew what he intended; there was only one thing.

"Oh hell, yes, you are," he said, and, without hesitating, he shifted his grip and, in the next moment, I was slung over his shoulder and his big hand came down hard on my too recently punished ass.

"Owww! Let me go. You're fucking crazy, Lake. Let me go!"

"What did you think you'd find, anyway?" he asked, walking through the living room and opening the front door all while I pounded on his back.

"I don't know what you're talking about. Let me go!"

It was dusk as he walked me across to the bad girl's room. He'd left the door unlocked and pulled it open. As soon as he stepped inside, I gripped the frame with both hands, refusing to let go.

"Please stop this, Lake. I haven't done anything. I swear. I haven't done anything."

"No?" he asked, turning, prying my fingers from where I held on for dear life. "No?"

Once inside, he carried me directly to the bed and set me down on it, the contact making me flinch. I glimpsed the strap hanging nearby.

"Please, Lake, I swear. I haven't done anything," I said, tears already beginning to fall as I took in the room, the open drawers, the suitcase.

"Give me your hands, Lily."

I felt the hope drain out of me when I saw the photograph with its cracked glass on the dresser. I looked up at him. He wasn't even looking at me, not at my eyes, at least. He was too far away.

"Please, Lake. I'm sorry. It was an accident."

"Your fucking hands, Lily!" he snapped, making me jump.

I held them out to him.

"Who was she, Lake?" I asked as he re-bound me. "Your wife? You're wearing a wedding ring in the photo. Where is she now?"

"Shut the fuck up."

"Did she leave you? Did you scare her away? Is that it?" He lifted me up to hook my wrists high enough over the bed that I was forced to kneel with my arms stretched overhead. He then tore the T-shirt I'd been wearing from me, stripping me so I was naked once again.

Why I didn't stop there, I don't know, because he still wouldn't meet my gaze. Fury came off him in waves, a hot rage too raw, too fresh, burned like an inferno in his eyes.

He wouldn't speak to me; he wouldn't even look at me.

"Did you hurt her, too?" I finally blurted out when he had reached the door.

He stopped then. For a moment, all I could hear was the sound of my heartbeat, the whirlwind of my thoughts until he finally looked at me. The glare with which I was met turned my blood to ice. He picked up the duct tape and tore off a piece, stalking toward me, filling me with terror. He gripped the hair at the back of my head and yanked it back, hurting me.

"Are you going to shut the fuck up or am I making you shut up?"

I only stared at him without speaking, without even opening my mouth, hoping it was enough of a message that I'd be quiet. After a few moments like this, he balled up the piece of tape.

"She's dead. She died because of people like you. Like your father. She's fucking dead, Lily," he said, his eyes now as red as mine, shiny with unspent tears. "Satisfied?"

He held me like that for a long moment, and we simply looked at each other until a tear slid down my cheek. Without another word, he let me go, turned, and walked out the door, leaving me in the dark room alone, cold and afraid.

I laid my forehead against my arm, and as if the heavens were sympathizing with me, I heard the first roll of thunder moments before a heavy rain began to fall, pelting the roof, the one darkened window. I tried to focus on that sound, tried to lose myself in it. But there wouldn't be any of that for me today.

Lake Freeman had been married. He had loved his wife. I could see that even now and his pain over her death was still raw. I wondered how long ago she'd passed away and knew from what he said that the cause of death was drugs. This was an impossible situation. Impossible. He'd punish me now for causing him pain, and, in a way, I wanted him to because as stupid as it was, as little sense as it made, I didn't want to hurt him. I didn't want to cause him pain.

* * *

I alternated between standing and kneeling to ease the strain on my shoulders and arms, willing him to come back and punish me just to be freed from my bonds, but when I heard the key slide into the lock, I stiffened, eyeing the strap, fearing his fury.

His footsteps were heavy as he walked inside. I turned my head just a little, not wanting to make eye contact, and I watched as he patiently and with great care repacked a few pieces that he'd taken out of the suitcase and zipped the thing. He then rose and took that as well as the photograph, out of the room.

I heard the sound of him opening the door of the truck and panic set in. Was he going to leave me here like this? He slammed that door shut and opened another. When I heard him start the engine, that panic reached a whole other level.

"Lake!" I called out, watching as headlights moved along the forest floor. "Lake! Come back!" Again I tried, knowing he wouldn't hear me over the sound of the truck. There was no way. When I heard him switch off the engine, I felt relief. Relief. Bound as I was, awaiting his wrath, his punishment, I felt relief that he wouldn't leave me.

If that wasn't fucked up, I wasn't sure what was.

"Lake?" I asked, my voice more quiet this time. I watched the open door, using the headlights of the truck to see any movement in the otherwise dark room. It was a moment, but soon, his form shadowed the doorway and I exhaled. "My arms, Lake. They really hurt."

"I imagine they do," he said, his voice quieter than usual.

"I'm sorry. You know I didn't mean to do anything wrong. You know that, right?"

He walked inside and this time, closed and locked the door behind him, switching on a light. Something in his eyes was different now, not hard so much as hurt. Hard might have been easier. I could hate him then.

"Lake?" I asked as he moved closer. "What are you doing? Are we leaving?"

"Not leaving yet, Lily," he said, setting a bottle of olive oil on the nightstand. He reached up to check my bonds.

"They hurt," I said.

"Mmm." He checked the second wrist but left me bound and went to lean against the wall instead.

"Lake?" He remained as he was, staring at me. "What are you doing?"

"I'm thinking about your ass, how raw it is. How much a fresh strapping would hurt, possibly break skin."

"Please don't use the strap on me again. Please, I said I was sorry and I am. I really am. I've been good. I didn't know, Lake. I really didn't."

Instead of speaking, he reached for the strap and took it from the wall.

"Please Lake!" I called out, twisting my bottom away from him as much as I could. "Please don't whip me. I'll do anything. Anything. Please!"

He stood looking at me, his gaze stone. He tested the strap against his thigh, making me jump.

"Turn around, Lily."

I shook my head vigorously, rising up on my feet now, yanking at my bonds in a ridiculous effort to free myself.

"Get back down on your knees and turn around, ass to me," he said, testing the strap again.

"Please, don't do this. Please," I begged, kneeling again, wanting to show him that I could submit, that I *would* submit, hoping for some mercy from him. "I'll do anything, please Lake," I said, not quite giving him my back fully.

He considered me for a moment then set the strap down.

I exhaled, my body relaxing a little. "Oh, thank you. Thank you."

"You may not want to thank me just yet," he said, reaching to undo my bonds. But instead of taking them off, he unhooked them from the higher ring and attached them to a lower one, one that had my forearms resting on the pillow of the bed so that in my kneeling position, I was crouched down with my face inches from the bed and my bottom high in the air. "Keep your head down, ass up," he said, taking the lid off the bottle of oil.

"What are you going to do?" I asked, some part of me already knowing what he had in mind as he climbed up behind me and settled between my knees. I remained still, my head down, my knees wide, my ass up, as he had instructed. The first drops of oil sliding down the cleft between my bottom cheeks had me closing my eyes even as my pussy leaked, my clit throbbing in anticipation.

"There are so many ways to punish disobedience," he said, pouring more oil. "Endless, really." I heard him unbuckle his belt then take his zipper down. I dared turn, looking first at his cock, then at him. He was watching me and he kept watching me as he poured a generous amount of oil onto his palm and began to coat his cock with it. I licked my lips, my mouth suddenly dry. His cock, thick and hard and entirely too big, stood ready, the tip of it brushing one buttock as he dripped more oil onto my ass.

"I'm not sure that's only the oil slickening that hot little cunt of yours, Lily," he said, his attention on my sex for a minute before returning to my face. Holding my gaze, he brought one finger to my back hole. "But it's not that cunt I'm interested in tonight." His greased finger pressed against my bottom hole and with the olive oil as lubricant, it wasn't long before he penetrated the tight ring.

I gasped.

"No, tonight, I think I'll fuck this little virgin asshole of yours." He pressed farther and my muscles all tightened. "So many ways to punish bad girls," he said, twisting his finger inside me then pulling out and pressing in again, smearing oil inside me, readying me to take his cock.

"Please…" I begged, but for what, I wasn't sure.

"Please fuck you? Is that what you want to say? Please

fuck my ass, Sir, is how that should go. Try it for me."

I shook my head, holding my breath when he pulled his finger out, poured more oil onto it and, adding a second finger, pushed in again, too hard, too fast, the intrusion burning from the inside.

"It hurts," I managed, my eyes watering, wondering which was worse, the strap or this.

"An ass fucking can be very pleasurable," he said, thrusting once more with his finger. "But it can make for one hell of a memorable punishment too." With that, he pulled his fingers out and gripped my hips hard, pulling my bottom cheeks wide. "I'll give you a hint, though. If you bear down and push against me, it will go easier on you. And I won't lie to you. This will hurt you much more than it will hurt me."

"Please don't, Lake," I squeaked, trying to pull away when he pressed the head of his thick cock against my back hole. "Please not there."

"You had no right to go through my things," he said, ignoring my protests, pushing his cock against my resisting back hole until finally, between the oil and the pressure, it opened to take him, the wide head of his cock stretching my asshole too fast, calling a cry from me.

"Don't do it, please," I tried again, but he ignored me, his thick cock pushing through my resistance, burning me. This was happening. He was going to fuck my ass to punish me. "Please. Please not hard. Please." I pressed my face into the bed my hands fisting handfuls of the pillow now wet from my tears.

"You had no right to touch her clothes," he said, as if he didn't hear me at all, his cock claiming more of my ass, taking inch by painful, burning inch. "Our photograph."

"I'm sorry. I didn't know. I swear," I cried. "You're really hurting me, Lake."

He paused for a moment, retreating a little, perhaps giving me a moment to adjust. But that wasn't it because with his next two thrusts, he reclaimed every inch he'd retreated and more.

"Almost there, Lily girl," he said, one hand coming around to rub my clit. "I'm about halfway in." As he said it, he began to move inside me again, claiming more of me, and when he began to rub my clit, I found myself laying my face down into the pillow, my eyes closing, the pain and the pleasure mixed, confused. He kept rubbing while his cock moved slowly in and out of me, claiming more of me, burning but then, after that burn or in spite of it, my ass stretched to take him, his fingers sliding easily along my wet pussy.

He worked slowly until I was moaning beneath him. I felt his thighs touching mine as both his fingers and his cock stilled. "There," he began, a slow movement of his hip accentuating his words while he took his fingers from my clit and set both to either side of my pussy, pulling me wide. "I'm in, baby. Are you ready to get your ass fucked, Lily?"

My response was a low moan. I looked over my shoulder at him. He had brought me to the edge, the sensation of pain, of fullness, and, most importantly, of his dominance over me, taking me out of my mind and fully into my body, fully absorbed in pure sensation.

"You like getting your ass fucked, don't you, Lily?" he asked, pulling out and thrusting so hard that I cried out. "I think you'd like it better if you'd be allowed to come, wouldn't you?" He thrust again and my eyes went wide at the assault. "But this is punishment." He pulled out slowly, dragging his cock from my depths before plunging in hard, pain the dominant of the sensations now even as pleasure whispered along its edges. "And bad girls don't get to come, do they?"

He moved his hands to my hips, lifting me higher, and, with the next thrust, pushed me to lie flat on the bed, his full weight on top of me, his cock fully and deeply seated inside my ass.

It was what I needed, all I needed, that contact with the

rough blanket on the bed rubbing against my clit, him moving faster in and out of my ass, making me moan as my muscles closed around his cock and I came with a violent shudder, the orgasm different than any I'd had before, leaving me shaking, hot and cold at once, his cock still while my ass throbbed around it, taking me out of my mind.

I don't know how long it was before I opened my eyes again but he waited for me to move, to make some sound before drawing me back up to my knees, his cock still firmly rooted inside me.

"Bad girl," he said. "You like having me in your ass, don't you, Lily?"

When I didn't answer, he slapped my hip hard.

I gasped, too ashamed to answer.

"Say it. I want to hear you say it." He smacked again, ignoring my cries. "Say it!"

"I like…" Another smack. "I like having you inside my ass. I like having you fuck my ass."

"Slut. Lift your ass to me, bad girl. Offer it to me. Beg me to fuck it." He slapped my hip hard and fast while he spoke, three quick smacks, and as sensitized as I was now and as tender as my ass was from my recent strappings, I called out, doing as he said, burying my face and thrusting my ass up to him to be fucked.

"Fuck me, Lake. I want you to fuck my ass hard. I'm begging you to fuck my ass."

And he did — he fucked me harder, his fingers working my clit, calling two more powerful orgasms from me. My ass burned as he used it, his own groans loud behind me. Sweat fell onto my back as he thrust harder and harder, our breathing ragged, the sounds in the room lewd, obscene even until finally, he stilled, his cock swelling, throbbing, releasing streams of hot cum deep into me.

We were both breathless when he collapsed on top of me, his hands still gripping me, his face against my neck, his sweaty body against my own. We lay like that for some time until finally, he slowly slid out of me and rolled onto his side, taking me with him, holding me to him.

CHAPTER 13

She was so warm, tucked in against his body as she was. He watched her as she slept, her head on his chest, her mouth open slightly, showing a hint of white teeth. He gently stroked the appealing curve of her naked hip, feeling the roughness of her skin where he'd spanked her, strapped her. She'd have a sore bottom tomorrow once again.

The little light that did make it in through the blacked out window had waned, dusk long since past, the room shrouded in darkness, the air cool, still scented with the smell of sex. He'd come too close, way too close to losing his control with her. The hurt...had been too much. So strong. But she hadn't known, couldn't have known. He'd told himself that as he'd fucked that curvy little bottom, watching the glistening shaft plunge and retreat between those red cheeks, their contours congested with strap marks swollen red and purple.

He'd strapped that bottom harder than he'd intended, but there was something about her, about the way she responded to being under his thumb, the way she softened and yielded under the punishing strokes, that drew him to her ever more.

Like a predator to prey.

But which was which here? As he'd pulled her trembling body close, for the first time, he'd wondered. She had a power over him, and though on the surface the dynamic appeared to go only one way, he knew better.

She was binding him to her as surely as he'd bound her wrists. The only open question left was whether or not she even knew it yet.

Lily had to be punished, though. And her hard assfucking was only the beginning. He'd made some progress with her, surely, but she still needed to learn, needed to see that he was both the beginning *and* the end. And everything in between.

Hell, it might even keep them alive, even as he feared his black heart might already be doomed. Every beat leading it one closer to its end, an end nearer than he wanted to even think about.

He thought she might still be asleep as he stroked the wild tangle of her beautiful hair. Someday he'd like to hold her quietly and play with those dark, silken locks, the soft weight of it falling through his fingers.

Someday.

Turning over the possibilities in his mind, he wasn't sure which path he'd choose, until the very moment he uttered the words.

"Why did you do it, Lily?"

He whispered it, lest he wake her from a slumber he knew she needed. Especially considering what lay before her.

"You couldn't leave well enough alone, could you?" His fingertip coursed slowly down the ridge of her pretty nose. "No matter what I've told you, what you've already been through, you just…couldn't help it."

Lake sighed in the dark, her head rising and falling on

his chest with the sounds of his breathing. He knew she wouldn't like it one bit, but he was equally as certain she needed it.

Her breathing was soft and slow, sleep shielding her from her ordeal, if only temporarily

"You're going to be punished, Lily."

Her body stiffened instantly against him, her breathing suddenly stopping.

So much for her being asleep.

He caressed the weight of her bottom cheek, his hand easing over the still-warm, swollen marks left by the strap. She sucked in a pained breath.

"Not here though, bad girl. Your bottom's had enough, for now."

"Please, Lake," she whispered, huddling closer to him. "No more."

He caressed her face, touched those soft lips.

"No more pain, Lily. But you're going to learn what happens when you look at something you shouldn't. Curiosity has a price."

He sat up, drawing her with him, holding her close. "Stay here," he said, standing.

Lily pulled her knees up, hugging them, those bright liquid eyes peering up at him in the darkness.

"I needed…to know. I'm sorry. I didn't want"—her gaze slid away, and she lay her cheek atop her knees—"to hurt you."

"You didn't, Lily." Lake straightened, pulling his jeans on, trying to ignore the fact that his cock was already swelling once more at what was to come. "But people like your father, the people he worked for…*they* did. They took everything."

He went to the closet, to one of the boxes he was sure she'd already looked through. There it was, at the bottom folded neatly under the files. A manila envelope. Perhaps she'd dismissed it, assuming it was yet more paperwork. He closed the closet, the envelope tucked under an arm, then turned to her. Her gaze alighted upon it immediately, her dark brows furrowing.

"Close your eyes, Lily."

"What? Why?" Her body folded in on itself tighter, her gaze flicking from the envelope back up to him. "No, Lake."

"Still don't understand, do you?" He pointed to the wall, where the dreaded strap hung, waited. "I said no more pain, but maybe you need more?"

Her head shot up, and she swallowed hard, the whites of her eyes showing. "No...okay. I'll do it. Please, don't hurt me."

Her eyes closed then, a tear slipping from under the lashes, dashing down her cheek, leaving a wet trail that glistened in the low light of the room.

"Good girl."

Opening the envelope, the folded black cloth slid out, soft against his palm. He put one knee on the mattress next to her, the blindfold stretching between his hands. When the fabric was laid over her eyes she tensed, a small, frightened sound coming from deep in her throat. He tied it snugly, carefully lifting her hair to ensure no strands were caught in it. She was going to be wearing it a while.

"Please, don't do this..."

He stood up, gazing down upon her trembling form. "Each time you lament not being able to see, I want you to remember what happens to girls who stick their little noses where they don't belong. Got me?"

"Lake, I don't—"

"Got me, Lily?"

She bit into her lower lip, hard. "Yes, Sir."

"Good." He walked around the bed, her head following the creaking of the floorboards. "I want you to lie down — and think. I'll be back soon."

He waited until she finally obeyed, her head making little spasmodic movements from side to side as if she could somehow evade the blackness of the blindfold. Lake touched one of her hard little nipples, tweaked it into even greater prominence. Her mouth came open a moment then her lips went tight.

"Over on your belly."

"Lake, please!"

"Just do it. I'm not going to spank you — unless you keep talking back."

"Yes, Sir," she murmured, turning over, the springs of the mattress stirring. He retrieved her leather manacles and slapped them back on quickly, binding her wrists fast before her shock had time to wear off. "This is so you don't get the idea that you can pull the blindfold off when I'm not around."

"How...how long?"

Smart girl.

She knew as well as he did that he couldn't keep her arms bound like that forever. Lily was already figuring, already planning, wanting to know how long she'd need to hold out, to endure.

"Long enough, Lily. How long depends on you." His cock was fully hard now, throbbing angrily. "You start being a good girl for me, doing what you're told, and maybe we'll take those off. But it's not happening until I can trust you to leave that blindfold alone. I want you to learn your lesson, bad girl. And we're going to take the time we need to make sure it sinks in."

He rolled her over onto her side, pulling the blanket up and over her naked, enticing form. He left her breasts uncovered, though, simply because he could, because it somehow emphasized her vulnerability, her femininity exposed to him, subject to him.

His.

With the final, sweet vision of her trembling lips and a tear slipping from beneath the black blindfold, Lake shut the door behind him.

* * *

Lake loved the sense of anticipation that surged through his muscles as he unlocked the door, as he imagined what her reaction would be. Would it be fear, or excitement? Did she crave it as much as she dreaded it? He wondered if she still hated him.

No matter what her mind might say though, her lithe, ever-responsive little body had certainly stopped hating him long, long ago.

Swinging the door open, he let what little evening light there still was in the sky into the room, a narrow strip of illumination falling upon the naked form of the bound and blind woman. Lily shivered, though whether from cold or fear he couldn't tell.

Her gorgeous dark nipples stood up just the same, either way.

He strode in, plunging the room into near darkness once again as he shut the door. He didn't need a light for what he had planned for her. Indeed, the absence of it fit his dark mood, the lust that surged up within him each time he visited his bound captive.

The same captive he should never have allowed himself to care for.

Too late now, Lake.

It wasn't too late to enjoy her for what she was though. His.

Utterly and completely, if only for a short, finite time.

He intended to make the most of it, until fate and circumstance decided to finally snatch her away from him, just as it had taken from him every woman he'd ever loved.

Love? This isn't love, Lake. This is...

"Possession," he muttered, pulling the folded leather from the pocket of his coat.

"What?" The slender column of her throat worked as she tried to look toward the sound of his voice. "What did you...?"

But he didn't say anything more. He knew it was what

she wanted — him to communicate. To acknowledge her as anything other than, something more than, the owned thing he needed her to understand she was becoming. The sooner she came to grips with it, the easier things would go.

And until that time, until she *really* understood, well, he'd slake his lusts with her in every way he'd dreamed.

"Lake, what are you...what are you doing?"

He unbound her hands, but only long enough to snap the length of leather to them. He tested the strength of the stainless steel snap, the polished metal gleaming in the low light. Then he drew her by the wrists off the bed, her bare feet slapping against the floorboards as she stood.

"I...what are you going to do? Talk to me, for God's sake. Please..."

But he simply shook his head at her, even though he knew she couldn't see it. His silence spoke loud enough for the both of them.

He backed her up against the wall then, the length of leather dripping down to the worn floor, dragging behind her like the menacing length of a serpent. His hand settled around her throat, and her breath caught, her body growing perfectly still, only the faintest trembling coursing through her muscles.

He grasped her under her chin, turning her head this way and that, admiring the slender neck, the delicate jaw, the flawless clarity of her skin. He tasted the softness of that skin then, kissing her along the line of her jaw, her breath drawn in and out in quick bursts. His hand coursed down the flat expanse of her belly, his fingers dipping into the liquid heat already gathering between the lips of her cunt. He yawned those soft petals apart, the spicy, clean scent of her sex filling his nostrils, his cock already a steel-hard bar in his pants.

Soon.

He took up the length of leather, and she cringed back ever so slightly, as if she feared he'd strike her with it.

She remembered her strap.

Lake smiled to himself as he threw the length of leather up toward the ceiling, looping it over one of the embedded steel hooks he'd originally intended to hang tools from.

Now he intended to hang something much more precious and valuable from that hook.

Drawing her arms up, he tied off the leather once he had Lily up on her toes, her belly sucked in below the heaving ribcage. He traced fingertips along the line of each rib, and she shuddered again.

"Please Lake, don't…don't hurt me."

It was so hard not to talk to her then, but he bit down the words before his tongue could speak them. Instead, he laid a finger over her lips, that touch saying as much — or more — than any words could. He kissed the corner of her mouth, a soft press of his lips to hers, and she relaxed slightly. He caressed the muscles of her arms as he felt for the tension, ensuring she was at least tolerably comfortable.

Then he gazed down at the plump lips of her sex, tracing the closed seam with his finger. He could feel her trembling beneath his touch, yet her hips eased forward, subtly at first, then blatantly as he took the finger away. He smiled at her then, though she couldn't see it behind her blindfold. He collected the wetness from between the lips of her cunt, and brought it up to her mouth, painting her lips with it then waving it under her nose. She licked the proffered finger quickly, almost greedily.

He could wait no longer, though, slapping at her inner thighs. She understood the message, spreading her legs as far as her position allowed. Next time, he'd have to secure her ankles to something too. He wanted her spread wide. Waiting. Surrendering.

He stroked her smooth, bare mound. She'd stopped talking, knowing by now her words were useless, perhaps acknowledging that her dripping cunt and impossibly hard little nipples betrayed her real feelings. He slapped her mound once, then again, harder, making her yelp. The skin flushed pink, immediately.

Freeing himself from his fly, he stood close to her, the broad head of his cock nudging the sodden, swollen labia. Lily grew still, her breath coming quickly, frantically, as he drew the head of his cock up and down through the slit of her sex, worrying the hard clit at each upward stroke, then gliding down once more. The tendons at her inner thighs stood out as she tried to spread wider, letting her wrists take more of her weight, her toes barely brushing the floorboards.

Good.

Lake drove up into her in one hard, brutal thrust, Lily crying out. He held himself close to her, breathing in her scent, letting her fear and lust and conflict wash over him, even as her cunt rhythmically squeezed him. Far from fighting him, she clutched him fervently, her heat and wetness engulfing him, welcoming him, whether her words — or her own mind — wanted to or not.

Lake took up a hard, steady thrusting, plunging and retreating within her, building up a faster and faster rhythm, until she panted, her breasts bouncing up and down with each punishing stroke into her heated depths. He grasped her under her arms, holding her still as he fucked her, and she clasped her legs around his hips, letting him feel some of her weight, allowing her the leverage to grind her hips against him as he moved.

"Lake…ah God, Lake. No…please, let me."

He ground a thumb down over her hood, slicking it back as the shaft of his cock thrust below. He exposed the bright red clit, rubbing it harshly, making her buck against him still harder.

"Oh my fucking God!"

But he didn't let her go over yet, instead leaving her clit, and holding her hips, reaching around and slapping her bottom as he thrust, a growl in his throat growing louder as she responded to each blow, squeezing his cock harder, her juices dripping from his swinging balls.

He grunted each time he pounded into her, cranking her head back to expose the soft, vulnerable throat to nips of his teeth, his kisses along her neck feverish, animalistic, tasting her sweetness, the smoothness of her flesh.

She was his now, right or wrong, and they both knew it.

Lily hissed, her teeth gritted together as his fist closed tighter in her hair, holding her still as he slapped her bouncing breasts, right, left, then back again, until those tight nipples were a deep red, little moans drawn from her lips at each sharp blow, his cock plunging deep the entire time.

He touched her clit again, growling at her.

It was all she needed, her hips bucking over and over, her screams echoing in the small room, her legs clasping him so tight he could barely move his hips. He rode her until her screams became breathless moans, her legs loosening then falling back to the floor as he pulled out.

"Lake…"

He pumped his cock quickly, looking down at the inflamed sex, groaning as his orgasm took him over, thick, pearly spurts of semen arcing through the air, crazed lines of viscous seed laying across the bare mound, a rope of it dangling from between her legs, semen mixing with the flood of liquid almost dripping from between the swollen, well-used labia. His vision faded to white for a moment as the hardest spasms rocked him, then he was finally spent, laying a palm across her chest, between her breasts, leaning against her lest his legs collapse.

Lily's head drooped then, her cheeks coloring beneath the black of her blindfold, her mouth a quivering O, her lips bitten a bright, inflamed red. Lake drew in a sharp breath as he touched the head of his cock to her mons, spreading the glistening semen over her plump mound until it shone with wetness. He wiped his cock on her tender inner thigh, leaving a bright trail of his seed across her skin.

He would've liked to teach her to clean his cock properly after he'd fucked her, but there wasn't time for that now. Instead, he tucked his cock back into his pants and lowered her back to the floorboards. Her legs gave out as he unhooked the strap from the hook, catching her before she could fall.

Lily murmured incoherently as he carried her back to the bed. A fresh tear broke from under the blindfold as he drew the sheets back up her naked, trembling body. He smeared the tear across her cheek with his thumb, making sure she knew he'd seen it, then brought the salt of it to his tongue, the taste making his newly spent cock begin to stir once more.

Something would have to be done about that blindfold though. He knew Lily well enough to know she'd almost certainly remove it when he wasn't there. He pictured her frantically pulling it back on as his key rattled in the tumblers of the lock.

He fingered the light switch as he stood in the doorway, looking over at her one last time.

Yes, it was time to show the disobedient captive that there were worse things than blindfolds.

* * *

I waited until I was sure he was gone. He could have been standing in the room watching me for all I knew. Semen dried on my skin, on my belly, between my legs, but at least he hadn't spanked me. The tenderness had finally faded and I could sit again without having to lean to one side or the other.

Certain I was alone, I brought my hand to the blindfold and pushed it up to my forehead, scanning the room quickly. It was so dark anyway, I don't even know why he blindfolded me. The only light at all was that sliver beneath the door and the slightly lighter black at the window he'd painted.

My eyes adjusted and I pushed the blanket off. Taking one of the bottles of water he'd left me, I went to the 'bathroom' and felt around for the towel he'd left behind. I poured some water onto it and cleaned myself. I smelled of sex, of him and me. I needed a shower badly but the thought of it was in the background somehow. It wasn't even the idea of escape that kept me busy anymore and that scared me.

Whatever he was doing was working.

Once the bottle was empty, I made my way back to the bed and sat down, touching to make sure I could easily pull the blindfold down when he returned.

My belly growled. The last thing I'd had was one of the protein shakes. I hated those and he kept feeding them to me.

I couldn't keep track of the time but I must have been in here for a few days. I stood again, stretching my arms over my head, twisting from side to side, moving into a yoga sequence I knew well, but after about five minutes, I gave up and sat down, my eyes hot again with tears. It wasn't working. Nothing was working.

The darkness was driving me mad.

Pulling my feet up from the floor, I scooted back to the corner so I could lean against the wall. I sat like this for a long time until that little bit of light from the window and the sliver of it beneath the door disappeared and the room was pitch black. I hugged the blanket to myself, no longer able to not take stock of things. Weight like a brick lay heavy in my belly, and I rubbed my palms over my face, my eyes. This was sick. What was happening to me, what he was doing to me was wrong. Sick. My wanting him in spite of that though, that was the sickest of all. I'd read those books where kidnap victims became emotionally attached to their captors and before this, before Lake, I thought I understood it. It made sense to me, as awful and unbelievable as it sounded to any sane, normal person. But now, now that it was me, now that he had me here in this dark room without running water, without even a toilet, coming in, using me, fucking me or feeding me, and my waiting for the next time the door would open and he'd return, it was that that made me truly understand, know what it meant not only with my mind but in every fiber of my being.

I felt, in one word, hopeless, but at the same time, his presence, his simply being here with me, would call things up, would make me feel things I shouldn't feel, I didn't understand. And as much as I wanted to hate him, to try to fight or at least resist, I wanted more for him to return. I wanted to hear the key in the lock. I wanted him to talk to me, even if it was a one-word command. Even if it was an order to get the strap. I wanted him. I needed him.

Without thinking, I reached over and switched on the lamp by the bed. I needed to cover my eyes for a minute, but once they had adjusted, I sat back again and waited, my eyes on the door, my heart in my throat. I waited for him, the strap hanging on the wall an omen in my periphery, but even that I didn't care about. At least he'd be here then.

But when, after I don't know how long, I heard a loud click and the room was plunged into darkness again, I jumped to my feet, hugging the blanket around me, running to hide in the darkest corner of the room. I listened to the sound of Lake's heavy boots coming up the front steps, the slight sound of the key in the lock louder than Manhattan traffic at rush hour. The door opened and there he stood, a flashlight in his hand, the residual light of it letting me see the hard look on his face, reminding me when the light shone in my direction to reach up, fingers scrambling to pull the blindfold back down over my eyes.

He made some low sound of disapproval and slammed the door shut behind him. I pushed my back into the wall, my knees already bending into a squat as he approached, my one hand still on the blindfold, the other clutching the blanket to me.

"You wanted me to come, Lily?" he asked, closing his hand over my arm and hauling me to my feet. "Well, here I am. Let's have some fun."

"No, Lake!"

He pulled me toward the bed, stripping me of the blanket as he did.

"I'm sorry! I just…"

"Bad girl," he said, tugging the blindfold off my face and tossing me face down onto the bed without any effort at all. "This what you want?" he asked, hauling me higher on the bed and taking the strap from the wall. "You miss me? You want some attention?"

I fought him, trying to get away even though, really, that was what I wanted. I wanted his attention. And I was getting it.

"Please, Lake. I'm sorry."

He pulled me up then, bringing his face inches from mine. "Actions speak louder than words," he said, the light of the flashlight he'd set on the dresser illuminating our corner so I could see his dark eyes boring into mine. "I'm going to teach you now once and for all to do as you're told."

I had no words; my mouth was dry, my body trembling as I looked into his eyes, knowing I was getting what I wanted and some sick part of me, even knowing what would come, still wanted it.

"No bonds. Go ahead and fight. I think you need this," he said, rolling me over onto my belly, his knee digging into my low back as the strap came down hard across my bottom.

He wailed on my ass. I screamed and fought, kicking my legs, flailing my arms, needing the fight more than I realized. He kept on with the strap, though, putting me back in place when I'd manage to get far enough away, not speaking while he strapped me, his breathing as ragged as mine as we fought until, finally spent, I stopped and reached up to take hold of a rung on the headboard and surrendered to it. I dug my nails into my palms when he moved his knee from my back and delivered the final strokes, fast and hard in one line, leaving my ass on fire before the strap hit the floor. The weight of the bed shifted as Lake knelt behind me, between my legs, his fingers gripping my hips to drag them upward.

"You're fucking wet, Lily," he said after closing his hand over my sex. With that, he drove hard into my pussy, making me suck in a breath and arch my back up to him. With his cock buried deep inside me, he laid his torso over my back and gripped a handful of hair, dragging my head up and back, his face so close to mine that his sweat dripped down my cheek. "I think you like this. I think you like having your ass strapped hard."

I shook my head. "No. Lake, I need…"

"I know what you need," he said, tugging my hair harder before pulling out of my cunt and this time, slowly pushing in again. "You need a good, hard ass fucking again, don't you?"

I shook my head no, but it was a weak effort. His hand in my hair hurt but I lifted my hips higher, wanting him to fuck me, any part of me.

"You shake your head no," he began, releasing my hair and straightening, pulling his cock out of my pussy. "But look at you."

Two fingers drove hard into my ass causing me to call out in a raspy cry. He dipped his cock one more time into my wet cunt, pumping his fingers twice into my ass as he did before removing them and lining the head of his cock against the tight passage.

"Please, Sir."

But what was I begging for? I wanted this. I wanted him inside me, inside my ass. I wanted him to punish me, to make me come, to wear me out, to stay with me and finally, to hold me when it was done.

He didn't speak again. Instead, without any gentleness, he pushed his cock into my ass, forcing it to stretch too far too fast, hurting me as he pulled out a little and thrust again, seating himself fully within three strokes, holding there while I breathed hard, pushing against him, willing my body to adjust, to open. I slid one hand down between my legs and he didn't stop me when I closed my fingers over my clit, the tips brushing against his balls as I rubbed, the muscles relaxing a little as pain and pleasure mixed and Lake began to fuck me.

He fucked me hard, he hurt me, made me cry out, but it wasn't wholly pain. And I came. I came with this thick cock stretching, spearing my ass ruthlessly, my hand soaked with my own juices until finally, I felt him swell within me. He thrust twice more, hard, his own sounds desperate and wild until his cock pulsed within the contracting walls of my ass, filling me to overflowing before we collapsed, his heavy weight on top of me, my hand still clutching my cunt, his cock still inside my ass.

* * *

Depriving her of sight was much more arousing than he'd ever anticipated, and he kept her blind far longer than he'd planned. He knew he couldn't resist her long, but he'd tried to distract himself long enough in the house to put together the bug-out pack he knew they'd need soon. He even pulled open the ammo case, and the gun safe — knowing he'd need all the firepower they could carry. But not even thoughts of impending death could keep him from looking toward where she lay, could keep him from gazing out the window at the guest quarters.

Finally, unable to resist any more, his cock an iron bar in his jeans, he went back out to her. She'd been half-asleep, but, at his grunted command, she'd lifted her hips, her cheek against her pillow. As he'd slid into Lily's wet heat, her long moan had been half fear, half lust. He'd taken her without a single word, a slap to her still-pink bottom, his only acknowledgment of the enjoyment of her body, the plundering of her charms.

Between visits to let her drink some water, to make her eat from his fingers, and trips to the bathroom, he'd left her in that room, alone, naked, bound, and blindfolded.

She was learning.

That night, he pulled her to her knees with a fistful of her hair, presenting the aching hard erection to her soft lips, and uttered the first word he'd allowed her in almost twelve hours.

"Suck."

Yes, Lily was learning indeed.

CHAPTER 14

Naked, he left me on my knees in the dark room on the hard, cold floor, want between my legs, his taste in my mouth after I'd swallowed what he'd shot down my throat. He'd said one word to me, exactly one word, and I'd knelt before him and opened my mouth like a good girl, and done as I was told: I sucked. I sucked his cock as if I were starving, and, in a way, I was.

I wasn't sure how long I'd been here. He'd fed me a few times but I couldn't keep track.

He wouldn't talk to me, not unless uttering commands to suck or get on all fours constituted conversation. I clambered to my feet and lay back down on the bed.

In a way, being here, in this room, gave me a sense of security. It was ridiculous, but as long as he kept me here, kept me in darkness and fully dependent on him, in a way, I belonged to him, and I was safe. I stopped thinking about everything else. None of it mattered in here, and it was, strangely, a relief.

Captive, Mine

I ate when he fed me, I sucked when he put his cock in my mouth, and I lifted my ass to him when he fucked me. I felt raw from the fucking but my cunt dripped for him, clenching around his cock whenever he took me. I was greedy for orgasm and wasn't even sure how I felt about that anymore. I should hate him, but all I hated was that he wouldn't talk to me.

The lock turned then and the door opened.

"Lake?"

Nothing but the sound of the forest before the door closed again. It was nighttime and the scent of something delicious had me sitting up, swallowing, my body hungry for hot food, for meat.

He dragged a chair across the floor toward me.

"Knees," he said. One word, cold and impersonal.

I obeyed instantly, sliding out from beneath the sheets and to my knees, sitting on my heels. When I'd spoken before, begging him to talk to me, he'd gotten up and left. I'd screamed after him but nothing came of it, and, if he was training me, it was working because I remained an obedient captive, kneeling before my captor, my master.

I swallowed again as the scent of meat wafted to my nose, salivating for it, not even ashamed of my base reaction. Was he going to taunt me with it? Sit here and eat fresh food while I knelt at his feet, hungry? Then it came, the first morsel. The scent and warmth of it had me opening my mouth. I inhaled as I closed my lips around it, licking his fingers with the mouthful, nearly crying as I chewed the tender flesh and swallowed quickly, opening immediately for more.

"Chew, Lily, or you're going to make yourself sick."

I nodded, my mouth still open, taking a second, greedy bite, forcing myself to chew, even though all I wanted was more. I opened again, waiting for the next bite, but he put a cold bottle to my lips instead. I twisted my face away. I wanted food. I wanted meat.

He chuckled. I hadn't heard that in...had I heard that

ever?

He placed another morsel on my tongue and fed me until I was sated after that, until I sat back, my belly finally full for the first time in a long time. It was then I felt something at my neck, and I drew back, afraid.

"Bad girl."

His tone wasn't harsh but it did bring me to heel. Bad girls got left alone in the dark with no one to talk to.

"What are you doing?" I had to ask, I had to try to engage him. I'd eaten now; he couldn't take the food away anymore.

The thing wrapped around my neck and he pushed my head down, my hair falling forward while he worked over me. It felt heavy, not in weight, but its foreign presence.

"What is it?" I asked, knowing all along. I touched the collar tentatively. "Lake...Sir," I dared once again to speak when he attached something to the collar. "Please talk to me. I'll be good, I promise, just talk to me now, please."

"Close your eyes, Lily."

I obeyed, remaining still while he slid the blindfold over my eyes again.

"No—"

"Hands and knees," he said, interrupting, tugging on my new leash.

Whimpering, I followed him, knowing why he'd put a leash on me when I heard the door open. The night air chilled me instantly and I stopped even while trying frantically to take in a breath of fresh air. But he tugged and we went, me crawling alongside him out the door.

"Two steps down, Lily."

We moved slowly while he held my leash, me wondering what he had in store for me.

"I'm cold."

There was no answer for a while as he "walked" me farther from my room. "Then you'll be quick. Here." He stopped, finally answering as he tugged on my leash. "Squat. This is your bathroom break."

Heat flushed through me, embarrassment at this new order. I turned my face up to where I knew he stood, and shook my head no.

"I'm wearing a jacket so I'm fine. We'll be here until you go and if you don't, we'll do this another way. It will be even more embarrassing then. Be smart."

"Please don't make me."

Nothing. Not a sound. I shivered again and rubbed my hands over my arms then touched his leg. "Please Lake...Sir...talk to me. I didn't mean to go through those things. I didn't mean any harm. Please talk to me now."

Again, nothing. Looking away, I positioned myself, forcing myself to relax enough to go, trying not to think of him there while he watched me in this most private moment, glad for the first time for the blindfold that hid me from him.

"Good girl," he said, before clicking his tongue, signaling me to crawl once again. "I'm going to give you a bath in the house now. Your reward for doing as you were told. Are you understanding this yet, Lily? Have you figured this out yet?"

The smooth wood of the porch was welcome on my palms and knees and when he opened the door, the warmth of the house almost made me smile. I crawled forward, eager now.

He closed the door. "Stay." It was an order, and I obeyed, sitting back on my heels. I heard his footsteps recede, then the flow of water filling the tub sounded like music to my ears.

"Sir?" I asked when he returned.

"I'm going to take your blindfold off now. It'll take a minute for your eyes to adjust."

I nodded, waiting as he took it away. The sight of him was fuzzy for a moment before I had to close my eyes again, the light too bright after too long in the dark. He waited while I rubbed them and slowly, I opened them again, blinking fast while they adjusted.

I looked up to find him watching me.

"I'm sorry. I'm really sorry. Can I come back here tonight please? I don't want to be out there anymore. I'm really sorry."

Without a word, his fingers hooked into my collar and raised me up by my neck while he squatted down. My heartbeat picked up at his violent handling of me, but my need to get closer to him overrode any fear, or at least equaled it.

"I expect you to be on your absolute best behavior for the rest of the time we spend together. When I say jump, you start jumping before you even ask how high. When I say sit, you drop to a seat wherever you are. When I say suck, you open your mouth. And when I tell you to get the strap, you get it and you bend over and offer your ass for punishment, understand?"

I nodded frantically, desperate to be back here and not in the bad girl's room. Desperate to be back in his good graces. "Yes! Yes, sir. Yes."

He looked at me, his expression stern, and I really looked at him. It had been so dark in the other room that I'd not seen his face in the days I'd spent there. He hadn't shaved in a while, the stubble along his jaw the beginnings of a beard now rather than a five o'clock shadow. His eyes looked different too, or maybe I was just really seeing them for the first time. There was more than hardness in them. Tenderness and hurt also took up space there, and worry furrowed his brow.

It was that that brought me back to the realization of why we were here in the first place. Of what was going on outside of the sanctuary of the isolated cabin where he'd brought me against my will, where he hid me from Randall and his men.

"Bath time, Lily. Crawl."

I swallowed. Now that I was without my bonds and in the light, part of me resisted, but I pushed through that, the knowledge of what would happen if I didn't obey too close. I crawled, instead, with Lake walking behind me, his whistle of appreciation solidifying to me my place as object or possession.

His object. His possession.

Steaming water had almost filled the tub, and Lake switched off the water. I couldn't wait to get inside it, feeling cold and filthy, even though he'd washed me — or more sponged me off — when I had been in the bad girl's room. I looked up at him, feeling very much the pet, and when he gave me his nod, I climbed into the tub, sinking into the too-hot water but not caring, needing that fiery heat to cleanse me as I closed my eyes and submerged entirely. I opened them underwater to find Lake waiting, watching me, his form massive from my angle. He didn't smile, but he didn't look angry either, and when I emerged once again, my eyes locked on the hard length of him barely contained behind his jeans, and my body began to prepare itself, as if it were conditioned to do just that.

We remained silent as he cleaned me. I was no longer desperate, blind, or hungry, and my mind began to work again, to recall the situation.

But I didn't want to think about that, not yet. The feel of his hands on me, a soapy cloth rubbing the intimate contours of my body leaving suds behind to cover my breasts, their hardened, dark nipples standing out among the white clouds. He had me on all fours, my bottom out of the water, and I simply complied, looking forward as he'd instructed while he, with soapy fingers, cleaned between my legs, my pussy, my ass, paying extra attention to my clit until I moaned. Then, with the greatest care, Lake shaved me, and, just as the water began to cool, he drained the tub and wrapped me in a towel before lifting me out of the tub to dry me.

I stood there, looking up at him as he did, looking at his eyes, his mouth, realizing I'd never once kissed him, really kissed him, not in a fit of passion, but differently. We'd done everything else, he'd fucked me every way possible and we'd tasted each other, but not once had he kissed me with tenderness, just to kiss me, and all I wanted in that moment was that, was that touch of his lips against mine.

He paused and I wondered if he felt it too when his gaze fell to my swollen lips as I licked them, preparing. Then, surprising myself, I stepped an inch closer and stood on tiptoe to brush my mouth against his, hesitating, lingering there, growing bolder and taking his lower lip into my mouth and sucking. My heart's beating was interrupted momentarily. His hand came to my waist, touching me softly while he opened his mouth. Power was exchanged again when that hand slid to the curve of my hip, taking possession, and his tongue dipped between my lips, my teeth, exploring, gentle, soft as he tasted me. I reached up to put a hand to his face, then wrapped that hand around the back of his head to bring him closer, wanting more, softness morphing into passion, lust.

But he stopped it then, breaking off the kiss, pulling my forehead to his lips and holding me like that for a moment, our breath ragged between us, the sound of my racing heartbeat the only other sound in the room.

It was only a moment of tenderness before his hand grew harder in my hair and he pushed me to my knees, releasing his cock and giving me that one command again:

"Suck."

I opened my mouth to take him and my pussy throbbed with need even as my heart saddened a little when that one little word put me back in my place, back on my knees before him while he used me, fucked me in any way he chose. That kiss may have affected me but it couldn't have touched him, even if I had seen tenderness in his eyes, even if there had been tiny kindnesses from him, even if there had been moments where he'd held me so gently, protectively even while he thought I'd slept. I had to remember that I only needed to survive this and I couldn't confuse dependence with anything more.

CHAPTER 15

The morning sun poured through the kitchen windows, the dirty glass rendering the sunlight into an almost hazy glow. Lake sat at the little table, the wood of the chair hard and cold against his ass. The coffee he brewed had burnt a little — the price of nodding off as it brewed — but the heat and the caffeine were welcome after another night on the lumpy, worn couch. He missed his bedroom, but he needed to be out in the living room. He could protect her better out there. He wondered why he didn't simply go to her, take her to his own room, make her lie with him, curl her warm, trembling body around his and take the comfort she so freely offered now.

But that would defeat the purpose of what he was trying to get through to her. So lumpy couch it was.

She'd taken the lesson to heart. He just wasn't sure if that was a good or a bad thing. He'd rather liked teaching her to obey. To comply, without question. She knew it now, down to the marrow of her bones. He hadn't had to punish her in days, and, even though a dark part of him was tempted to strap those plump buttocks simply for the pleasure of watching the lush flesh bounce and wobble under the blows, he'd resisted. As long as she kept it up, kept listening and behaving, he'd leave that strap hanging on the wall in the Bad Girl's room.

You need to stop wishing she wasn't so well behaved. And start thinking about how you're getting your asses out of this.

Lake looked up at the sunlight, the angle of it already lower. Cold weather wasn't far away, and winter at the cabin was a brutal, grueling affair he wouldn't wish on his worst enemy. Time was running out, and though the diversions were more than enjoyable…he knew a reckoning was coming.

And soon.

Sighing, Lake reached into his pocket, laying his cell on the nicked, faded wood of the table. He took a sip of the acrid, but still blessedly hot coffee, and leaned to the side, pulling out the pistol. Laying it on the table next to the phone, he stared at it then looked at the phone. Back and forth, one to the other.

You better know what the fuck you're doing, Lake.

He looked toward Lily's room. The morning light still hadn't reached the hallway, the shadows darkening the corridor such that he could only vaguely make out her door. Did she still sleep?

It would be better if she did.

Lake laid his left hand over the gleaming, polished metal of the M1911. He didn't even know why he still carried the old hand cannon. The Beretta was far more accurate, though without the satisfying punch of the .45 caliber Colt.

Somehow, holding it made him feel better. How far had he fallen when the only two things that made him feel better anymore were his weapons and the captive woman thirty feet away who'd still probably kill him if given half the chance?

No time for self-pity anymore, asshole. It's time to do what has to be done.

He lifted the pistol from the table, resting an elbow on the wood, turning the weapon in the sun, the light glinting off of it in blinding flashes. Lake looked down that hallway one last time.

"No going back from this, Lake."

His whisper seemed harsh in the quiet of the cold morning.

He picked up the phone, his thumb punching in the numbers fast before he thought better of it. Odds were good that the number wasn't even in service anymore, but it was worth a shot. A call from him would be unexpected — and he needed every ounce of surprise he could squeeze out of the FUBAR jam they were currently in.

Lake grunted at the sound of the call going through. Not disconnected after all. Someone picked up before the second ring.

"Bishop."

His raspy voice still made Lake's skin crawl. When he'd first met the man, he'd had no idea what Randall was thinking keeping such a scrawny, pimply-faced scumbag around.

Then Lake had witnessed what Barry Bishop could do with a gun...and a knife.

"Get your boss on the phone, Barry."

There was a pause, and an intake of breath. "This can't be you..."

"I'm waiting, asshole. Make me wait any longer, and I'm hanging up. I don't think the boss man would be happy to learn you'd jerked me off on the phone rather than putting me through to him."

"All right, all right. Wait a second!"

The line went quiet.

Lake's heart pounded harder and harder as each second ticked by. Did he expect him to call? Was he that far ahead of Lake? That the line hadn't already been disconnected…wasn't good news.

It said: confidence. That was never a good sign when dealing with a cold-hearted sociopath.

"Mr. *Freeman*. I was about to show Barry here the error of his ways in pulling my chain. I didn't believe it was actually you."

The man's voice was smooth and deep, ever relaxed, not so much as a syllable raised in anger or distress. Lake could picture the asshole right now, the jet-black hair, the bleached white teeth with the too-prominent canines, the deeply tanned skin as if he'd spent one too many hours out on the links.

And the eyes, like two points of black iron, as hard and pitiless as his soul.

If he had one.

"I'm going to talk, and you're going to listen."

Lake clutched his weapon tighter, relieved his voice hadn't cracked with the strain. He knew the next few seconds might well doom he and Lily both to a torturous death and a shallow grave.

"Now, Mr. *Freeman*, what kind of tone is that to use? We're all…friends here. Why don't you come in; we'll talk things over. I'm sure we can come to an agreement on—"

"Shut the fuck up, Randall."

The man made a sound on the other end of the line somewhere between a murmur and a growl.

"I still wonder, Mr. *Freeman*. Did you plan it from the very beginning? Did you enjoy her yet?"

"That rapist piece of shit is lucky I didn't take his little pecker as a souvenir."

Randall's laughter made Lake grit his teeth.

Thirty seconds alone with you, motherfucker. That's more than I'd need.

"My little mole in WITSEC…you surprised him. I told him I need people who can actually *complete* the job assigned to them. Someone like you, actually. DeSalvo is careless, and weak — stupid. You know, it's not too late to make things whole again, Mr. *Freeman*. You worked for me once — you can do it again. If you make the right decision here."

"I'll take my chances."

"Slim chances, Mr. *Freeman*. Slimmer by the day, I'm afraid."

The pleased sound Randall made sent chills down Lake's spine. Something wasn't right. Randall knew — *had* to know — that Lake had him by the short hairs. Lily was supposed to be Randall's trump card. The one thing neither the feds nor Randall had control over anymore. With Lily gone, so was any leverage the drug dealer hoped to hold over Emmanuel Cross.

The news should've sent Randall into a homicidal lunatic rage — he'd seen that side of Randall before.

And dead, broken bodies were always the result.

"Bring Ms. Cross in, Mr. *Freeman*. Finish the job I paid you for. I don't give two shits about what you did to DeSalvo. He's lucky I didn't put a bullet in his brain over his little fuck up."

"You're wasting your time, Randall. You'll never find us. The money you pay for those clowns. What do you call them again? *Associates?* You might as well set fire to it for all the good it's doing you."

Randall's low chuckle had Lake squeezing the pistol so hard his knuckles creaked.

"I'll put you in charge of guarding her, Mr. *Freeman*. Nobody else touches her. DeSalvo can go rub his prick up against some other whore. She's yours, and you can use her to warm your cock any time the mood strikes you. I'll even—"

"If you ever see me again, Randall, I'm the last person you'll ever see. Count on it."

"Why so upset, Mr. *Freeman*? Listen. You can just drop her off. Name the time and place. After, you can disappear. As long as you stay good and gone, we'll be square. I'll consider the money you stole from me...the cost of doing business."

Something's wrong, Lake. He's stalling for time.

"Give it the fuck up, Randall. I'm hanging up now."

"That place in Huntington Beach was a nice touch. Hiding in plain sight."

Oh fuck.

"Mmmm, you didn't think we'd find it, did you?" Randall's voice changed, the smooth affect gone, the rumbling menace of the thug loud and clear. "I didn't think we'd get lucky with the first one. So we used process of elimination. Your little beachside hidey-hole is a smoking hole, now. Cops might even think it was arson, too. Wonder who might stand to gain from a little arson, Mr. *Freeman?*"

"You fuck."

"The kid you had renting the place in Raleigh. DeSalvo says he'll live, but he's gonna be in the hospital for a few weeks."

Jesus Christ.

"Oh and the place in Montana? If you're there...well, you might have some company. And soon. Hell, they may have been watching it for days. Or not. I guess, well, you wouldn't know, would you, Mr. *Freeman?*"

Lake's mind reeled, his mouth suddenly bone dry. How? They had even less time than he'd hoped. If Randall was checking each one — and Lake would, were he in the cold-blooded killer's shoes — they might have...days.

For all he knew, Randall had every single safe house already pinched. Maybe he was just waiting?

"Bullshit. If you had a fix, you'd have already come for us."

"*Us*, is it?" He could *hear* the smarmy grin in the man's voice. "That little cunt's got you wrapped around your finger already, doesn't she?"

"Fuck you, Randall."

"Tell me something, Mr. *Freeman*. How does a man like you afford all of those properties?" Certainly not something you could afford on a SEAL's pay, is it?"

"I'm hanging up—"

"Of course not. But you see, Mr. *Freeman* — I *know*. I vet everyone I hire. Everyone, you hear me, you fuck? You thieving fucking *rat*. Eventually, we'll find the hole you crawled into, and you'll wish you'd taken the second chance you're about to piss away." Randall went silent a moment then the smooth, relaxed tone was back. "Last chance, Mr. *Freeman*. You know I never forgive anyone who fucks me over. But, for you? I'll make an exception. Drop her at the original hand-off spot. Just drop her — and make yourself scarce. Permanently. It'll be over. You can find another one of your holes and stay in it. That's it."

"She's told me everything, Randall. *Everything*. You think she's just Cross' spoiled daughter, don't you? Well, if you do, you're even dumber than I thought. She knows everything, Randall. Her daddy doesn't even know as much as she knows."

There was the slightest pause from Randall. "Is it Michigan, Mr. *Freeman*? Or the apartment in Vancouver? Where are you, *little rat*?"

He knew he'd gotten Randall's attention, the man's voice suddenly tense once more, his textured voice almost a growl. A pissed off Randall was a sloppy Randall.

It was all he had at this point. Lake hoped it would be enough.

"Emmanuel's the *decoy*, you murdering prick," Lake snarled, the rage filling him again, his vision tinged with red. "Did you ever consider that? Lily's the real prize — and you'll never find her."

Then Lake hung up.

It was all a fucking lie, of course. Lily wouldn't tell him jack shit, even if she did know something, but it might be enough to shake Randall just that little bit, get him thinking.

Get him doubting.

Lake stood, tucking the .45 back in his waistband as he

strode toward her bedroom.
It was time for Lily to make a phone call, too.

* * *

"Time to call your dad, Lily. Here, get dressed."

I sat up, rubbing sleep from my eyes. Lake stood over me with a mug of coffee in his hand. I looked down at the clothes he'd tossed onto the bed then up at him. His face told me not to say a word about it, and I didn't, knowing how hard it must have been for him to give me her clothes to wear.

"What time is it?" I asked, taking the coffee.

Lake sat down. "Early, but we've got a lot to do today."

"Um...okay I guess. What do we have to do? Did something happen?"

He hesitated. I could see he had something on his mind and when he mumbled a quick "nope," I knew for a fact he wasn't telling me something.

"Why do I get to call my dad all of a sudden?"

"If you don't want to..." He rose to stand.

"No. Of course, I want to, but I feel like there's something you're not telling me."

"Nothing you need to worry about. Come on, make the call, tell him you're okay. The sooner he testifies, the sooner this is done and the sooner we can stop running."

"You know we'll never really be able to stop running, don't you? I mean, I don't fool myself with the naive idea that once my dad's testified and Randall is behind bars where he belongs, that he'll just call it good and live out his days locked away in a prison in peace. That's not how he works. That's not how this will work. You and I will be on the run for the rest of our lives, Lake."

Lake ran a hand through his hair and walked to the door. "I know that, Lily. Now get up."

I finished the coffee and set the mug down before standing. There was a lot going on in my mind too. Questions I'd been able to keep at bay but that still nagged at me. "What's going to happen afterward?"

He looked at me, exhaled, and rubbed the back of his neck.

"I mean, after my dad testifies. What are we...what are you going to do?"

He stared at me for a long minute, and I couldn't make sense of why this was so important. Why I felt so anxious waiting on his answer.

"I'll disappear, like you will, if you're smart."

I looked at him, taking in the words he'd chosen, trying not to allow the disappointment to show on my face, not sure at all why I felt disappointed. It was the last thing I should have felt, wasn't it? I mean, I would be free again, free of Lake, at least. I did not entertain the delusion that I'd go back to my New York City apartment and pick up where I'd left off. That life was over. And I was sure as hell not going into the witness protection program, even if they put DeSalvo away with Randall. There were probably a hundred like that asshole, a hundred pricks who could easily be bought. I would disappear too.

I guess I just hadn't expected to have to do it alone.

"Where's the phone?"

He studied me for a minute, and I wondered if he, too, felt disappointed, but trying to read Lake Freeman was an impossibility. The man was like a vault, any emotion buried deep down, the tiniest glimpses of their physical expression fleeting at best.

"Inside."

"Okay. Let me get dressed first."

He nodded, picked up the empty coffee mug, and walked out of the room.

I snatched up the jeans and pulled them on. They were a near-perfect fit but for being a little short at the bottom. The navy-blue hoodie he'd chosen still had the tag on it. I tore it out and slipped it over my head, making a stop in the bathroom before heading into the living room.

Lake stood leaning against the counter, drinking coffee. On the kitchen table, he'd laid out two revolvers, one smaller than the other, both deadly. A few days ago, I might have made a run to grab one, but that thought didn't even cross my mind. Instead, I picked up the phone that sat next to the guns and looked to him for the okay.

"You don't tell him where you are, not the tiniest description, understand?"

I nodded.

"Tell him you're with me and that I'll keep you safe until he testifies. The sooner that happens, the better."

"Okay."

I dialed the private number my dad had given me, pulling out a chair and sitting down as I did. It rang twice, and a male voice came on the line. Although my dad was behind bars, he had different privileges than the other inmates. Different rules to live by.

"This is Lily Cross."

I didn't have to say another word before my dad came on the line, his relief almost palpable from this side.

"Lily?"

"It's me, Dad." Emotion I'd not expected to feel flooded me and I sat at the table suddenly sobbing, holding the phone to my ear, listening to my dad thanking God on the other side, laughing pitifully in relief. "I miss you, Dad."

"Are you okay, honey?"

I nodded, sniffling. Lake handed me a tissue and I took it, wiping my nose. "I'm okay."

There was a pause. "Where are you, Lily? Is there someone there with you? It's not safe for you to call me."

"You don't know what happened, do you?"

"What are you talking about?" A longer pause where I could almost hear my dad thinking.

"I'm with Lake Freeman."

"What the hell?"

"He saved my life, Dad. DeSalvo works for Randall. He was going to hand me over to him to keep you from testifying."

There was a pause while my dad processed. "You with him now?" he asked more calmly.

"Yes."

"He's not hurting you, honey, is he? I'll fucking kill the bastard if he touches one hair on your head."

I couldn't help but chuckle at that. My dad, my hero. Always coming to my rescue. "I'm okay. Listen, Dad," I began when Lake gestured for me to get on with things. "I need you to testify. Randall's looking for us, obviously. We don't know how close he is. The sooner you testify and he's prosecuted, the sooner this is over."

"Where are you? No, don't tell me. I don't want to know where you are. Put Lake on the phone for me."

"Okay. Hold on."

"Honey, I love you. No matter what happens, I'll do everything I can to keep you safe."

"I know, Daddy. I love you, too."

I held the phone out to Lake and took another tissue.

Lake's conversation with my father was brief, a lot of "yes, sirs" and "I understands." The conversation was one sided and I smiled through my tears thinking about how Daddy was probably threatening him with all kinds of awful things if anything happened to me.

If he only knew.

Lake hung up, shoving the phone into his back pocket.

"Ever shot a gun, Lily?"

* * *

It took us about an hour to walk to a clearing after a quick breakfast. Lake had determined I needed to learn how to shoot a gun, and I figured that wasn't a bad idea. We now stood with Lake explaining the various parts of the handgun to me while I listened, taking in as much as I could.

"Here, this one's yours."

I looked at him, still surprised at this change. Not too long ago, I was his prisoner. Now, he was handing me a pistol.

I took it from him, the metal cool in my hand. Although it didn't weigh much, it felt heavy to hold.

"All right, can you take the stance I showed you?"

I nodded and moved into position with Lake watching, my right leg slightly back, holding the pistol like he'd shown me and raising it, my right elbow locked, the pistol at eye level, taking aim.

"That's good, very good," he said, stepping closer, his body pressing against mine to adjust my position, the thick length of his cock unmistakable against my hip. I rubbed against it, unable not to. It had become my body's natural response to complement his arousal with its own.

"Pay attention, Lily," he said, squeezing his hands around mine.

I groaned my displeasure, his breath at my neck only making me want him more.

"Ready to fire?"

"Yes."

He held me close from behind while explaining how to take aim before pulling the trigger.

The sound startled me even though I knew it was coming and I wasn't prepared for the recoil. Lake chuckled at my response and set me up again, making me do it on my own several times until I got used to it, or at least as used to it as I was going to get. He moved off a little ways and watched, instructing me from a distance to adjust this or that. I had to admit, I liked the feel of it, I enjoyed the weight that had intimidated me at first. I could do this. I felt powerful holding the revolver, and I could protect myself. I wouldn't have to rely on Lake or anyone else.

"You're doing really well, just one more thing," he said, coming up behind me. "Hold it right there, a hair higher." He adjusted the level at which I held the pistol before his hands roamed down to undo the button of the jeans I wore. Without undoing the zipper, he pushed his hand inside, cupping my sex. I gasped in response as he ground himself against my back.

"There's something about a beautiful woman holding a deadly weapon in her hands that makes it possible for me to think about only one thing." He licked my neck then kissed it, his fingers working inside the jeans, making it difficult for me to hold any position at all.

"I think you're always...thinking...about only one thing." I turned my face, licking my lips as I looked at his before locking eyes with him. I wanted him to kiss me. I wanted him to kiss me more than I wanted him to fuck me and I wanted that badly. I'd never been a shy girl. I took what I wanted, at least I used to, but with Lake, it was different. Maybe that was why I wanted it so badly.

Eyes wide open, I kissed him, tasting his lips, his breath, and, to my surprise, he opened to me, letting me slip my tongue inside his mouth for a moment before everything shifted and he took over. Our bodies pressed against each other, my breasts crushed against his chest, one hand cupping my ass, the other at the back of my head while with his mouth, he took.

His cock stood like a steel rod between us and he walked me back a step, two, before we both fell to the ground, breaking the kiss. His eyes dark and lustful on mine, he wasted no time pushing my sweater up, baring my breasts, cupping them, squeezing them hard before scratching short fingernails over the nipples. It hurt but it aroused at once and I reached for the crotch of his pants as he pulled the zipper of my jeans down and tugged them to my knees.

I took his cock into my hands, smearing the pre-cum on its head, but when Lake's hands came to my hips, lifting me, turning me over onto my hands and knees, I resisted.

"No. I want you to kiss me. Please Lake, kiss me."

Without a word, his body fell heavy on top of me and his mouth once against crushed against mine. All the while, he shoved my jeans farther down my legs until he could position himself between them. He pulled back a little, his breathing hard as he lined his cock against my entrance. I reached to pull him back down. I wanted him to kiss me again, I wanted him, needed him, not to stop kissing me. But he held me down and watched as he thrust once, deep and hard, into my pussy.

"Ah. Again."

He didn't speak, only watched me while pulling out then driving into me again. "You like it like this, don't you, Lily," he said, kissing me again between words. "You like it when I fuck you hard. When I make it hurt."

I could only groan, holding onto him, lifting my mouth to his when he pulled away. The heat between us had me sweating even in the cold morning air. When I felt the slight change in rhythm, the thickening of his cock, I knew he was close, and when he gripped a handful of hair and forced my face up to his, I looked up at him watching me, watching me as he fucked me, watching me bite my lip hard enough to draw blood as I came. His fist in my hair only tightened when, with an almost animal sound, he, too, came, burying his cock as wave after wave of pleasure sent his seed deep inside me.

CHAPTER 16

He never imagined it would ever come to it, but Lake walked the perimeter. It felt good to have the M4 back in his hands again, even with the ghosts it brought back. The M4 was a chance, a choice, and maybe, just maybe, survival.

Down the last two hundred meters of the driveway he looked for fresh tracks, knowing that if he was lucky, the only two sets of tracks he'd find should be the fresh ones from his truck, and the old ones from the propane delivery he'd had a couple weeks before bringing Lily up there.

His luck had held.

Taking a right off the driveway, he plunged deep into the brush, then turned and dropped prone, scanning the driveway through his sight. If someone was going to move on the house, they'd do it now. If someone was there.

Randall was rattled, that much was clear. The rage Lake had heard in the drug dealer's voice said one thing above all — frustration.

The bastard still didn't have a fix on them.

True…until it isn't.

They still had time, but there was no way of knowing how much. The cabin was essentially off the grid. No power connection, no water connection, the driveway not marked on any map. It had, decades ago, been a hunting lodge, nothing more than a shack in which to get out of the snow for a few hours.

But it was a shack only his family knew about. An ideal fallback position. He never thought he'd actually *need* it.

Tracking along through the forest, he kept to a ridge line that had been thinned when Lake was still a young boy. It had filled in again somewhat, but the canopy had only grown healthier since then, leaving the understory little sunlight to work with. Consequently, the sight lines were quite good down the ravine. He didn't think anyone would be stupid enough to approach the house from such an obvious direction, but he knew paid goons weren't renowned for their intellect either.

DeSalvo wouldn't be that dumb.

Lake cut back to the north, the cabin to his south directly between him and the driveway. The terrain there was rocky, the brush much thicker, fit only for elk — and the suicidal. The ridgeline formed a long arc that encircled the cabin on three sides, leaving open only the gentle slope to the south from which the driveway approached. He hadn't realized it until he'd had the cabin built — they'd always hunted to the south as kids — but it had been a welcome discovery, making the site that much more defensible.

He took a knee at a game trail he knew led south, back to the cabin. The trail terminated at a sunken area at the edge of the ridge, a giant fallen log lying across the southeastern stretch providing good cover from anyone approaching from the direction of the cabin. It would have to do.

Skirting around to the eastern side of the cabin, he humped it as far as the brush let him, only turning back when the ridge disappeared into impenetrable brambles and fallen trees about 150 meters east of the cabin. Too close for comfort, but it was also the least likely avenue of approach.

Moving directly west, he came out on the driveway a hundred meters from the cabin. The terrain was exactly as he'd remembered it — far from perfect for bottlenecking any approaches, but better than it could've been. He had all the advantages — except the advantage of time.

Good enough.

As he double-timed it along the driveway back toward the cabin, he brought the carbine up, checking both sides through his sight. He didn't expect to find anyone, but he needed to know how many seconds he'd have for an enemy approach once Randall's men zeroed in.

He made it to the cabin far quicker than he liked.

It was time to get Lily ready too.

* * *

Lake found her standing at the window as he opened her door, the light from the hazy sunshine rendering her form into muted grays and whites. She hugged herself tight, turning to him, a question in her gaze. He'd decided not to bind her wrists this time. Lily needed a chance to behave on her own.

Relief flowed through him to find her safe and in her room, exactly where he'd left her.

The instruction with the pistol had been a test. He honestly hadn't been positive she wouldn't train the pistol on him and try to shoot him.

The blanks he'd loaded in the clip had allowed him to take that chance. Now, it would be another test for his wayward, beautiful prisoner.

"We're going for a walk." He extended a hand toward her. "Come on."

"A walk? Like *outside*?"

He nodded at her, beckoning her with his hand. "Daylight's wasting."

Lily froze for a moment, her gaze meeting his, and he saw something in those gorgeous eyes he realized he didn't like seeing anymore.

Fear.

"Jesus Christ, Lily, I'm not going to hurt you. But you need to see something. It's important."

"Why can't you just tell me?" She brushed a lock of dark hair away from her eyes.

"You're gonna have to trust me on that. It'll make sense." He took a step toward her. "Time to go."

He stood aside as Lily slipped by him, then paused, just inside the doorway. She glanced up at him, and he touched her cheek.

"Lake...I'm afraid."

He pulled her into his arms, and she clung to him tightly, a surprising strength in her limbs. He spoke into the softness of her hair.

"I know you're scared, Lily. We're doing this so you

won't be afraid anymore. Pay attention and follow my lead, and you'll be fine."

He tried to ignore his reluctance to release her from his embrace. Where once she'd have done anything to avoid being near him, now...it was something quite different.

Lake followed her out to the porch, and she blinked at the brightness of the light.

"Follow me, Lily."

He made for the game trail, stopping after a few steps into the brush and looking back to make sure she still followed.

Her slim form hung back at the edge of the forest, as if she feared losing sight of the sanctuary and light of the cabin property. He didn't blame her one bit.

"Come on, Lily. It's safe, but you need to follow me."

He led her into the forest, the shadows swallowing them up, the air cooler under the thick canopy. There'd been a time he wouldn't have trusted her to follow him a single step, but he hoped she would feel more secure with an open route back to the cabin.

Leading her to the sunken area behind the fallen log, he turned to her.

"Did you pay attention to how you got back here?"

Lily looked up. "I don't...where the hell are we?"

"About a hundred meters from the cabin." Lake kicked the hulk of the log. "Remember this. This is your rally point. Got it?"

"No. I have no clue what that even *is*."

Lake sighed. "If...something happens. This is where you go. This is where we meet up again if we're separated."

"I don't...is something going to happen?" Lily's eyes went wide, and she looked back toward the house. "You don't think he knows about this place, do you?"

"I have no idea, but Randall knows enough. This is just in case."

"Just in case *what?*"

Lake crouched down behind the log, pulling out the

bag hidden beneath the hulk. It was a padded, camouflaged gun case. He drew the zipper down and pulled the shotgun from inside.

"Jesus Christ." Lily backed up a step.

"Relax." He held up the gun. "Take this."

"W-why? I know — you showed me the pistol."

"A pistol's great for the cabin, but it's gonna be practically useless to you out here."

He dropped the case to the ground, holding the gun up for her. "Take it. You need to get used to handling this."

"That thing will knock me over." She crossed her arms over her chest, but took a step closer. "I can't use this."

"Yes, you can. Come on, take it."

For a moment, her eyes narrowed, flicking from the gun to him then back again.

Bad girl.

"That clever mind is always working, isn't it, Lily?"

Her mouth dropped open, and she looked up at him. "I don't…"

"Save it. Take the gun."

She finally took the weapon, but, surprisingly, she didn't hold it away from her body as if it were a dirty animal.

"Not your first time, is it?"

The lithe little woman was full of surprises.

"I've fired rifles before, but this isn't…the same thing. Is it?"

Lake chuckled. "No, it's not. I want you to aim it."

He didn't move, watching her closely, curious as to what she might try.

"Aim it at what?"

The barrel moved up, uncertain, but the meaning clear.

"Don't bother. It's unloaded."

She scowled at him, pivoting and aiming at the fallen log.

"Now, make sure that stock is tight against your shoulder." He moved behind her and cinched it firmly against her. "Like that. You hold it like a girl and the kick's gonna break your shoulder."

"Fuck you," she whispered.

He was glad she couldn't see his smile.

Lake moved to the side, pointing at her. "All you gotta do is get close, and pull that trigger. It's loud as fuck, so be ready for it, but it'll stop anyone coming at you. Got it?"

She pulled the trigger to a metallic click.

He stepped close, tapping the top of the receiver of the gun. "You see that red dot?"

"Yes."

"That's the safety — it's off — which is why you heard that click. If that thing had been loaded, you'd have just blown a hole in that log there."

He took the gun from her, slipping it back into the bag. "It's not loaded now, but after today, it will be. And it's staying right here."

Her gaze snapped to his. "You mean…?"

"Yes, you'll have a loaded weapon out here. That's the whole reason for doing this. This is a rally point. Anything goes down at the house, this is where you run. You understand me?"

"Lake, what the hell is going—"

"Understand me, Lily? This is fucking serious."

"Yes, okay! I get it." She looked down, hugging herself once more against the chill. "It's cold out here. Can we go back?"

He studied her, seeing her fear.

"Let's go," he said, leading the way back to the cabin.

CHAPTER 17

Two tense days had passed since Lake showed me the rally point and that shotgun. In a way, those days I'd spent in the bad girl's room had cocooned me from the terrifying reality of what my life had become. We were on the run from a drug lord who would kill Lake on sight and do God knows what to me if he ever caught up with us. Being in the dark almost seemed preferable because, as much as Lake scared me sometimes, I knew he wouldn't ever really hurt me.

Strange how that thought made the hairs on the back of my neck stand on end. I felt like Pavlov's dogs: think of Lake, link it to hurt, and I'd become aroused. There was something seriously wrong with me.

I glanced over at him sitting behind his laptop, wholly focused on the map he was studying.

It was raining again and although normally I hated rainy days, up here, I almost preferred it. It made me feel safer, which was stupid. I sat at the window watching it fall, listening to it. It was early evening and already dark beneath the heavy canopy of trees.

"Do you have some wine or something?" I needed something to calm my nerves.

He looked up at me and rubbed his eyes. "No, no alcohol, Lily. I think we should leave tomorrow morning. Early. We've been up here longer than I expected to be, but I don't want to take the chance on our luck running out."

I'd told Lake about the safe deposit box containing cash and a brand new identity for me, and the plan was to get me to it. We'd then have enough money to disappear. Maybe take that flight to the south of France after all. Together.

Jesus, what are you thinking?

What was wrong with me? Once I got to the bank, I could lose Lake and disappear on my own. That's what I would do if I were smart, at least. With a new identity, I could hide indefinitely —even *I* didn't know the name on the passport Daddy had had made for me — so there was no way Randall did either. I could rent a house and take an extended beach vacation. For a moment, I imagined the warm sand between my toes and the sound of the sea. I imagined being carefree in the sun, like I used to be. But, too quickly, those thoughts grew heavy. My dad would still be in prison, and Lake, well, Randall would never stop hunting him for his double cross, I knew that. He might give up on me once my dad testified, but Lake? Not a chance. And I couldn't think about him getting hurt.

"I've got the route planned out," Lake said, shutting down his laptop. He checked his watch. "I know it's early, but why don't you go to bed? I'll finish loading the truck so we're ready to take off. I'll have to wake you up around four o'clock."

"Four? That's middle of the night, not morning."

He shook his head. "Sorry, princess."

I wasn't a princess, and I *hated* being called one. People assumed it because of the way I looked, or maybe because

Captive, Mine

of having come from money. I didn't know but I didn't like it. It pissed me off. "It's not only princesses who don't like having to get up at 4:00 AM, jackass."

I got up and went into the bedroom before he could reply. I didn't want to hear another smart comment from him telling me who he thought I was.

A moment later, Lake stood in the doorway actually looking apologetic. "I didn't realize you were so sensitive. I'm sorry, okay?"

I shrugged a shoulder and tucked my hands behind my knees to swing my legs off the side of the bed. "Whatever."

"Hey," he said, coming into the room and sitting down beside me, taking my chin in his hand and tilting my face up. "I said I'm sorry."

"Okay." Then, "I'm not sure about leaving. Maybe we should stay here. I mean, if he hasn't found the cabin by now, chances are he won't, right?" I was scared, that was all there was to it. "They moved the trial up, which means Dad testifies sooner..."

"Which puts that much more pressure on Randall to find us faster. We can't stay, Lily."

I knew that already, didn't I? I nodded and leaned my head into his shoulder, my eyes warm again from tears.

"I'm scared."

"I know." He took my face in his hands. "I'm not going to let anything happen to you, understand?"

I nodded, a few tears sliding down my cheeks as I did. I was scared for me, obviously, but it wasn't just that. I was scared for him, too, and I had a bad feeling about this, about going to that bank.

"Maybe I can sleep next to you tonight?" After everything that had happened, he'd never once let me do that. We'd never actually spent a full night sleeping next to each other.

"Sure. Go get ready for bed and I'll get you tucked in."

"Thanks."

Natasha Knight and Trent Evans

* * *

"**W**ake up, Lily," Lake's whisper was startling, but he put his finger over my mouth to shush me. "We've got company."

My heart pounded. This was it; they'd found us.

"Get your shoes on and wait for me here. Stay low by the bed. Everything is loaded in the truck. I'll be back to get you, but if I tell you to run, you remember where you have to go?"

I did, during the day. "I think so." I hoped it wouldn't come to that.

He nodded and I slid out of the bed as he walked to the door, pistol in hand. I slid my boots on and crouched down low, watching him until he disappeared. The house was dark but the forest was darker. What if something happened, and I had to make it to the rally point? What if something happened to Lake and he couldn't? What then?

But I didn't have to think about it for too long because Lake was back. With a nod of his head, he gestured for me to come and I did, keeping low like he'd said before. He took my hand.

"They're on foot, but we're definitely not alone. Truck's around back, but we'll go out the side window. They'll have men on the doors if they're that close. If we're lucky, they won't notice we're in the truck until we're blowing dust in their faces, but remember to keep low, understand?"

I nodded, my heart in my throat, fear the only thing I knew. But it turned out I didn't know anything until we were half out the window and the sound of gunfire broke into the quiet of the forest. I screamed, and Lake pulled me the rest of the way out and pushed me to the ground so fast, it hurt.

"Rally point, Lily. Go!"

Lake shot his gun, three quick, terrifyingly loud pops, and I ran. I ran like I'd never run in my life. Gunfire lit up the night behind me like fireworks, but I only had to look back once to know not to look back again.

When he'd shown me the rally point, it had been full day. Now, in the dark, I was completely disoriented and freaked out with the war going on around me. He was one man against how many? Too many shots firing for me to know. I heard a man's voice calling to find me, and I turned to look back, seeing the light of two flashlights coming in my direction. Shit! I had to find the rally point! I had to get the shotgun, or I was finished. I turned and tripped over a rock, landing hard but scrambling to my feet quickly. My knee hurt, but this was life or death, and I had to keep going.

"She's here!"

Fuck!

I heard the truck roar to life then. Lake had made it to the truck! I had to get close enough to the clearing that he could pick me up, but how, with these men chasing me? I tripped again, screaming as bullets flew over my head, just missing me.

"We need the girl alive!" someone called out.

Lake turned the headlights of the truck on the men who were chasing me, grabbing their attention. They aimed their guns but Lake was faster, taking one man down while another got a shot that ricocheted off the hood of the truck.

"Lily, in!"

I ran toward the truck, my heart racing, my breath coming too short. Gunfire again as I yanked the back door open and jumped in. I'd barely closed it before Lake began to drive, getting one more bullet off, hitting the man who'd been so close to me. I watched his body jerk and then drop.

"Down, Lily. Christ, do you ever fucking listen?"

I'd forgotten. I dropped to the floor of the backseat as the truck bounced this way and that, driving over fallen logs and debris. I heard men cursing and more bullets and then Lake laughing. He was *laughing*.

Captive, Mine

"Lake?" I was frantic, my entire body shaking.

"Rally point, Lily. I thought you said you knew where it was."

"Is it over?"

"Stay down there, in case there's more men, but I shot their tires out so it should give us enough of a head start to disappear."

"Oh God. Okay. Okay, that's good."

"You hurt?"

"No. You?"

"Just nicked my shoulder. Fuckers can't even aim properly."

I peeked up over the seat to see the bloodstain on his shirt. "Lake, you're bleeding!"

"Stay down! Do as you're fucking told for once in your life, will you? Fuck!"

I dropped back down to the floor. "Does it hurt?"

"Flesh wound. It's fine. Rally point, what happened? You went in the completely wrong direction!"

"I was disoriented and had people shooting at me! You try to find a rally point in the middle of the woods in the night with people shooting at you!"

"Women have a shitty sense of direction, in general. I don't know why I thought you'd make it there."

"I don't have a shitty sense of direction. We're in the middle of the fucking woods, asshole!"

"All right, princess, calm down," he said, laughing.

"I told you, I am *not* a princess!"

After a few twists and turns, the ground became less bumpy, making me think we were on a paved road now.

"Can I come up?"

"Yes."

"Shouldn't you put the lights on?"

"Only if we want them to find us. There might be more out here." He looked over at me, scanning my body as I strapped my seatbelt, remembering that first day. "You okay?"

I nodded. "I think so."

"Good news is, we're ahead of schedule."

I looked at the clock. It was twenty minutes past 3:00 a.m. I smiled back at him, realizing he was trying to set me at ease.

"Thanks."

He nodded, his attention back to the road. "Let's hope for an uneventful drive."

* * *

We drove for almost two full days to get back into the city, stopping at rest stops along the way to freshen up but not taking a chance on an overnight stay at a hotel and surviving on coffee. He told me to sleep more than once, but I couldn't. I needed to stay awake with him, I felt like we were in this together now.

Lake circled the bank too many times to count before deciding it was safe enough and that we hadn't been followed. He was acting weird, quiet, but I decided it was because we were both tired.

"You ready?" he asked when he finally settled on a parking spot.

I nodded. "We can leave the car here," I said. "Leave everything behind and get a flight out to wherever."

He smiled and squeezed my hand, walking me to the bank. "We'll see. Let's get your passport and the money, first."

I nodded, but something was wrong. Off. I felt it. "Lake?" I asked, stopping in the middle of the busy street. It was late afternoon and sunny, so maybe not the smartest thing to do.

"Keep walking, Lily."

I walked, and to any passerby, we probably looked like a regular couple out on a regular day. But I could feel the hard metal of the gun Lake carried beneath his jacket. We were anything but normal.

At the bank, he opened the door, and I walked in ahead of him. Taking out my ID and the key to the box, I approached a woman who took the identification and told me to wait. Lake stood beside me, seeming anxious.

"I'll wait here for you. We don't want any surprises." His eyes were red rimmed.

"What's going on?" I asked when he wouldn't meet my gaze.

"Nothing."

"Are you angry? Did I do something?"

"Ma'am?" the woman called to me.

"Just a minute," I snapped, not meaning to. "Lake?" I hesitated. "You're going to be here when I come out, right?" My heart beat fast, and I opened my eyes wide to prevent the collecting tears from spilling.

His answer was written on his face, in his eyes. He took my face in his hands, and a tear rolled down my cheek.

"Shh. Don't cry, Lily," he said, wiping that tear and the one that followed away with his thumb. "You'll have a better chance without me now. You get yourself on a flight out of the country and take a vacation. God knows you've earned it. Keep a low profile until this is over."

"No," I managed, shaking my head, embarrassing myself as I came apart. "Please, Lake, you can't leave me to do this alone. I can't…"

"You can and you will. You have to," he said.

"No. Not anymore, not after…what happened."

He looked over my head, his fingers pressing on my face as he battled something inside himself. I watched the demons shadow his eyes, saw his lips tighten with resolve, and when he brought his mouth to my forehead and held there for the longest kiss, I knew this was goodbye.

"Ma'am, we're ready for you."

Lake looked at me, his eyes redder too. He reached down to hug me one more time, the scruff on his face scratching my cheek as his lips touched my ear. "Goodbye, Lily. Be safe."

I didn't say a word. Instead, when he pulled back, I stood in the middle of the bank, wiping my face with the backs of my hands, sniffling loudly while I watched him go. He didn't look back, not once, and I knew why. I knew it had taken all he had to walk out that door.

I turned to the woman, who politely ignored the state I was in, and, once I was alone, I broke down and wept fully at this sudden and unexpected loss of him, loss of the man who'd kidnapped me to save my life, who'd punished me and loved me mercilessly. And I knew he did love me. He had to. It was there in his eyes, and I'd never forget that look for as long as I lived.

I'd never forget Lake Freeman.

CHAPTER 18

For some reason, he'd expected waves. The teal-blue water of the Gulf of California was as calm and warm as bathwater.

Lake brought the cold bottle to his lips, the bitter, cool liquid of his beer washing over his tongue. The resort didn't really live up to the title, being more a huddle of modest homes, condos, and a couple restaurants crowded around the edge of a small cove. He didn't care that he was being "that guy," the *gabacho* lying on the blindingly bright white beach, beer in hand, hiding from the ghosts of his homeland.

Sure Mexico was a risk, but it would be the last thing Randall would expect — Lake hiding in the belly of the beast. The resort was almost exclusively North American expats, with a smattering of Europeans. The rest were rich tourists. That it was the largest concentration of Americans in the entire country made hiding there easier than he'd ever have believed.

There was one problem though, a big one.

Lily.

She'd opened a door to a part of him he thought had died with his wife. But it hadn't.

Lily had likely spilled everything to the feds. With luck, she'd forgotten him, buried it down deep, purged the memory of what they'd done, what they'd *been*.

But he'd never be able to forget her.

Why had he done it? He'd saved her...and taken from her in every way a man could take from a woman. From his captive. What did it mean that she'd responded to him?

It means Stockholm syndrome, you prick.

She'd simply been trying to survive.

Despite the shimmering heat of the afternoon, Lake shivered.

You became what you'd saved her from. So, did you really save her, Lake?

"Cerveza, señor?"

The waiter was so young, teens maybe. Fresh faced. Clean. Unsullied by corrupting desire, unburdened by the consequences of a life of bad and worse decisions.

"No, thanks," Lake said, pressing a bill into the boy's hand.

He grinned at Lake and stepped away, the white linen of his apron flapping about his legs.

There was a place in the Queen Charlottes he'd looked at last year, a place Lake thought might be perfect. He liked the rain, and it didn't get any rainier than off the coast of British Columbia.

Even though Randall had somehow sniffed out the house in Vancouver, this would still be far enough away it was unlikely to raise any attention. Besides, for the moment, anyway, Randall had a lot more on his plate. Lake hadn't killed all the men who'd found the cabin — not by a long shot — so it was a certainty now that Randall knew he and Lily had slipped away.

Lake picked up the paper — the resort somehow, miraculously, had access to several US newspapers — the story just below the fold something he was particularly interested in.

Terrence Randall Facing Trial on Numerous Federal Charges

"Burn, you sonofabitch."

Maybe when he finally saw the murderer hauled away in cuffs, it would finally feel over, even though he knew it wouldn't be.

Maybe the rain, and quiet, and solitude of the Queen Charlottes would help wash it all away. Someday the ache would ease, assuming he lived that long. At least seeing Randall in the clink would let Lake let her go. Finally.

A gust of wind galloped in off the water with an angry snapping sound as it caught the faded fabric of the umbrella shading Lake's table.

He raised the bottle, tipping it toward the water. "I hear ya', honey."

With Randall gone, the pain of Sara's passing would finally fade, if not at rest, at least avenged. It would have to be enough.

Lake waited until almost sunset to walk back to his room, his thoughts returning to Lily as he opened his door. He sat at the sliding glass doors as day slowly gave way to night, as memories of the past gave way to regrets about the present, dread of the future.

Without Lily there with him, perhaps his penance for what he'd done, for the choices he'd made. Life had a way of settling accounts. The knowledge that she surely must hate him by now did make it easier, or at least took away that illusion of choice, or options. Sometimes what we want lies behind a door our actions have locked tight.

The question was, what did she really want? And what was Lake prepared to do to give it to her?

It was idiocy, but how many nights had Lake laid awake in the sweltering dark, the AC off, the fan blowing the hot, weighted air over his skin? How many nights had he wished it were Lily there with him, in his arms, the choices, the decisions, the consequences no longer mattering?

All that mattered was that she'd be there with him. Confronting a future neither had chosen, a future neither wanted to face alone.

Lake was hiding from it, from the unavoidable, awful, terrifying truth of it.

And it wasn't just from the long reach of Terrence Randall.

You have to tell her, Lake.

Lake turned away from the muted cries of the seabirds, the inebriated, chattering expats stumbling along the beach outside.

As fatigue weighed heavily upon him, deep in the sweltering night, sleep finally found him, the vision of Lily's beautiful, luminous eyes the last thing he saw before the dark swallowed him up.

CHAPTER 19

Even though winter in the south of France was moderate, I welcomed the warmth of Mexico. Discarding my wool sweater, I left the windows of my rental car down and began the long drive to the house where Lake had been living for the last year.

I had done what I had always wanted to do after Lake had left me at the bank that day. I had booked a flight to Nice and rented a small house on a hill in Chateauneuf, near Grasse. I had been living quietly there for a little over a year. My hair was finally growing out from the pixie cut I'd sported at first, and it now just touched my shoulders. It was also finally back to its natural color and not the caramel blonde I hated but had to do to alter my appearance.

The first months, I'd been scared. Sleep was a luxury then, and I had kept mostly to myself. I spoke French fluently, which helped, and people seemed to respect my privacy.

In the last four months, though, things had changed,

starting with Randall's arrest. He had been tried, finally, and, earlier this week, I had learned that my dad's testimony would put him away for life. Along with the details of Randall's verdict and sentence was an article crediting DeSalvo with leading the roll-up of the cartel and speaking of his promotion because of it. DeSalvo, whom I still remembered sitting in the car next to me, sliding on his leather gloves to keep his prints off my body as he did whatever he wanted to do to me before handing me over to Randall. I wanted him punished. It was unfair that he not only got off scot-free, but was rewarded as well.

I'd learned long ago that life wasn't fair, though, and sometimes a compromise was the only alternative. I couldn't punish DeSalvo, but that didn't mean I'd roll over either.

My father was out of prison and had started a new life in the witness protection program. We still had contact — that had been a non-negotiable part of my dad's deal from the start — but I felt like it was time to pick up my own life again.

After all this time, I would finally see Lake.

I'd found him six weeks ago. It hadn't been easy, but being the daughter of a crime boss had its benefits and I wasn't above taking advantage of them when I needed to.

I'd done a lot of soul searching over the last year. At first, I chalked up my feelings for Lake to Stockholm syndrome and forced myself to think about the bad things, the punishments, the humiliations. I wanted to forget him and hating him was the closest I could come to that...except that I didn't hate him.

And forgetting him wasn't working.

Those days in the cabin, in the "bad girl's room," they had changed me. It was like they'd chiseled off this layer to expose a part of me I'd never known existed, but that was more real than anything else, made me feel more alive than I'd ever felt before. In a way, even though life had been easier before Lake, I didn't want to go back to that, to that version of myself. I couldn't. I loved Lake. It took a lot for me to finally admit that and know that it wasn't some residue of the trauma that had become my life in those weeks.

It was real. I loved him.

The sun began to set as I neared my destination in the small fishing village. The setting was beautiful, the spot he'd chosen off the beaten path. I slowed to check the GPS on my phone and continued onto the unpaved road closer to the cove. A beat-up old work truck was parked by the small house and, from this distance, I could see there was a light on inside.

I slowed the car, my heart beating faster and my stomach nervous as I neared the place. What would it be like to see him again? What would I feel? What would *he* feel? I smiled. He'd be surprised, that's for sure.

But would he be happy to see me?

I glanced in the rearview mirror, suddenly questioning what I was doing here, so far from home, on a hope and nothing else. What if he *wasn't* happy to see me? What if he didn't feel the same? What if he'd long forgotten me? And worse, what if he wasn't alone?

"No."

I straightened up and drove the last part of the road to park next to the truck. Dust kicked up around the car, and my face felt grimy and hot from having driven with the windows down the whole way. Brushing nervous fingers through my hair, I climbed out of the car and walked on heavy legs toward the house. I tried for a friendly smile as I neared the door, my heart pounding in overdrive as I neared it, but before I even reached it, the door opened.

I stopped, hesitating, the smile I'd attempted fading because it wasn't Lake who stepped out to greet me from behind that door. It was a woman, an older woman. She looked at me, her expression one of worry. A child of about ten peeked out from behind her, wrapping her arm around the older woman's waist. She was too young to be her daughter. This was her granddaughter, at least.

I said hello in Spanish, extending my hand in greeting, my presence obviously making her nervous.

"You're American?" the young girl asked, her words accented heavily.

"Yes. You speak English?"

"A little."

"I'm looking for someone, I thought I had the right address," I started, showing them the address I'd written out.

The old woman said something and the girl answered her, but I couldn't follow.

"This is the address," the girl said, looking at my paper. "But my family lives here now."

I looked at the old woman who studied me, saying something else to the girl.

"Are you sure I have the right address? Is it possible—"

"What's your name?" the girl asked.

"Lily. Lily Cross." I hadn't used my real name in a year. I'd been Lynette Moning, as my new passport read.

"Wait here," she said as the older woman went inside.

The last of the sun would be gone in minutes, and I watched it disappear into the horizon. The water shimmered, and I inhaled a deep breath of salty sea air, trying to listen to the sound of the water rather than giving in to the panic rising in my mind.

The old woman returned, holding an envelope. The girl took it and handed it to me.

"We are to give you this. He left it if you ever came."

She looked at me, the concern in her ten-year-old eyes too heavy, making mine fill with tears as the realization that he wasn't here, that I was too late, dawned on me. A few moments passed while I just looked at her, unable to glance at the envelope I held.

The old woman spoke to me this time, gesturing toward the house.

"She says for you to come inside. It's late, and there's

no hotel here. It's not safe for you to drive alone now. You may spend the night."

I looked down at the envelope, my hands shaking. He'd written Lily across the front of it. No last name, just Lily.

"Come." It was the old woman this time, and I went with her, my body feeling numb as I walked into the tiny house with its broken-down furniture, the smell of food cooking, the sound of the television playing an old American Western in the background. I sat on the couch, and the young girl brought me a glass of water. They then both went into the kitchen, leaving me alone.

I opened the envelope slowly, barely feeling the sharp sting of a paper cut smearing a drop of blood across the top of it.

Inside was one folded sheet of paper. I opened it, not sure what I expected, what I hoped for, and I read it without feeling a thing even as my whole body seemed to shake.

Lily,

If you're reading this then you're doing what I hoped you wouldn't. Even though I know you can't help being who you are, the rebellious, strong, frustrating bad girl, you still shouldn't have come. If I were there with you now, you'd be getting more of what hung on that wall in your room at the cabin. I'll leave it at that just in case Alejandra took a peek at this. I don't think she will though. She's a good woman.

What happened — it was wrong. Even though we felt something, it was wrong. We both know it. But I'm not sorry I did it. I'm not sorry I met you. And I'm not sorry I saved you.

I'm going to save you one more time though, and this time it's saving your life in more ways than one. Leave me, leave the memories. Let them lie. What you think you want isn't what you'd find. Let time swallow me up, erase me from your mind, free you from what cannot be.

Lake

* * *

It had been three days since I read that letter, and I still shivered at the memory of it, my hands growing cold, my chest feeling tight, my belly heavy. Lake was gone. It was finished. I wouldn't try to find him again. He didn't want me to. But I'd still do this one thing for him, even if he never knew I did it.

Although I was now back in New York, it no longer felt like home. It was like that life before, my life I'd been so attached to, was so far away, it wasn't even real anymore, and I didn't miss it. I packed the last of my things into my suitcase but left the bag in my hotel room. It wasn't quite five-thirty in the morning. I would have time to return before my flight back to France. Slipping on my heavy coat, I picked up the small pistol I'd set on the dresser and tucked it into my pocket, knowing that if I needed to, I would use it, that knowledge scaring me a little.

But I knew the kind of man I was dealing with. DeSalvo wouldn't hesitate to hurt me if he thought he could get away with it. I needed the reassurance of the weapon in my pocket until I convinced him hurting me would be a bad idea.

Checking my watch, I pulled a tight wool hat over my head and left the hotel. It would take me half an hour to walk to our meeting point, a public street that would offer just enough protection for me to deliver my message. I kept my hands in my pockets as I walked, the thick envelope on one side, the pistol on the other.

I was first to arrive at the meeting point, or so I thought until DeSalvo walked out of the small café on the corner sipping a coffee and holding a second one, looking too relaxed for my comfort. I'd hoped to beat him there. I was still early. But I should have known better with a man like him.

"Ms. Cross," he said when I neared. "I got you a coffee." He held the second cup out to me, the gesture catching me by surprise, which I knew was exactly what he wanted.

When I'd contacted DeSalvo, he'd been, for at least one tiny moment, caught off guard himself. I'd told him I wanted to meet, had given him some idea of what it would cost him if he didn't come alone, and hoped he had believed me, but I realized now that I could have been wrong. He could have men stationed all around. I'd been naive. He seemed too calm, too collected, too confident. I needed to shake that confidence, and fast.

"No, thank you," I said.

"Suit yourself," he said, setting the cup on a high windowsill.

I noticed then the black leather gloves he wore, the same ones he'd put on that night while I'd watched. It made me shiver, but I fisted my sweaty hand around the pistol in my pocket and forced myself to breathe.

"Randall will be pleased to know you're back in town."

"I bet he would be, except he's not going to find out."

"And why would that be? Certainly you're not naive enough to think just because he's behind bars the organization has been wiped out."

"No, not that naïve," I said. "I grew up a part of that organization, remember. I am my father's daughter. Underestimating me would be a mistake." I paused, letting my words sink in, knowing he didn't really see me as a threat. Not yet. "I know what you would have done to me. I know what kind of man you are."

He didn't seem at all ruffled by that. In fact, he checked his watch and sipped his coffee, his posture relaxed. "Get to the point, Ms. Cross. It's cold out here."

"You're here, DeSalvo. It means you know I'm a threat to you."

He chuckled at that, the coffee sloshing out of the side of the cup with the movement. "Hardly. I figured if you had the balls to actually show up, well, then I'd—"

"Shut the fuck up," I said, my lips curling in my dislike of this man. I wanted this over. I wanted to get as far away from DeSalvo as I could. And I needed to make sure he stayed away from both me and Lake.

I pulled the envelope out of my pocket and held it out without quite offering it to him. A small twitch of his eye when he saw it told me he wasn't as confident as he was trying to make me believe, and that bit of knowledge strengthened me.

"I want you to know, first of all, that should anything happen to me, any strange sort of *accident*, I have a letter waiting to go out to the authorities as well as to your superiors detailing exactly what happened the night of my disappearance, telling them who you moonlight for, who pays into that bank account of yours in Moscow." I hadn't wasted the last year. I'd been doing my homework and dug up as much dirt as I could on DeSalvo. I had enough to put him away, but jail wasn't where I wanted him. I only needed him to *know* the power I held over him.

Now I offered the envelope to him. "This copy is for you, in case you'd like to have a look."

He took it, his eyes on mine until I let it go. When he opened the flap to look inside, I had him. I knew it.

He turned back at me, his gaze flat and cold. "What do you want?"

"I want a lot of things, but I'll settle for one from you: stop your search for Lake. Forget about him, forget he exists."

His eyes narrowed and he cocked his head to the side, studying me, leaving my confidence of a few moments ago on the verge of evaporating. "My business with Lake Freeman is between him and me. You worry about your own pretty little self. I have nothing with you. I didn't even see you here today, in fact."

"Not enough. Leave Lake alone. Stop searching for him, and you'll get to stay out of jail. Unless you miss your buddy Randall, that is."

His grin unnerved me. This meeting needed to be over, and fast.

"You found him, didn't you?"

I tried to keep my expression neutral, but my reaction to his comment was physical.

"Do we have an agreement?" I asked. "Or should I"—I reached into my purse and pulled out a duplicate envelope, this one stamped and ready to be mailed—"drop this at the post office a few doors down?"

His expression hardened. "You wouldn't."

"Why wouldn't I? What have I got to lose?"

He studied me, but this time, I was able to keep my calm. I had the upper hand, and we both knew it.

"That's fine, Ms. Cross," he said, dumping the rest of his coffee onto the street, some of the cooling liquid splashing onto his shoes. He then crushed the paper cup before tossing it too. "As far as you and Freeman are concerned, we have no more business together."

I smiled while he tucked the envelope into his pocket, all the while my heart racing.

"You shouldn't litter," I said, gesturing toward the cup on the street.

He looked pissed, and I couldn't say I didn't like it.

"Good-bye, Ms. Cross."

"Good-bye, DeSalvo."

By the time I'd said it, he was too far away to hear.

CHAPTER 20

He grew very still at the sound of the lock tumblers moving.

Sitting in her living room, cloaked in shadow, he'd waited, every second wondering why the fuck he'd done this — and knowing there was nothing else he could've done. Not anymore.

She stepped in, snapping on the foyer light, warm illumination showing the softness of her hair, her face every bit as beautiful as the one he'd seen every night in his dreams. Unwrapping the burgundy scarf from her long, slim neck, she turned to close the door and threw the deadbolt.

"Hello, Lily."

She froze, her back to him, the thin leather strap of her purse a diagonal line down one shoulder of the form-fitting black coat. Her hand eased down to her purse. She was careful to keep it in front of her, but he knew what she was doing. It made him smile.

Lily spun on him, the pistol trained toward the sound

of his voice, though she'd have shot over his shoulder if she'd fired.

"Get your hands up and show yourself." Her voice was firm but tense. She was scared, but that steel he so admired was still there. Good.

"You need to aim that about eight inches to your left."

The black barrel instantly moved to him.

"That's better."

Her brow furrowed, her eyes going wide.

"Is it...?" The pistol wavered, but the barrel didn't drop.

That's my girl.

"Your house was ridiculously easy to break into. You need a nosy *voisin* watching out for this place."

The barrel of the gun steadied instantly, pointed directly at him. Her eyes narrowed. "Show yourself, or I start shooting. I'm bound to hit something."

He flicked on the light next to the chair, the little chain on the switch rattling against the metal base of the lamp.

"You're still holding it like I taught you."

Lily's face went pale, and this time the barrel of the gun did drop. "*Lake?*"

He stood, but she raised the gun again.

"I...you shouldn't be here. You said—"

"I said you needed to forget. But no matter how hard I tried, no matter how many days went by, *I* couldn't forget." He took a step closer, but she backed away.

She was thinner than he remembered her, her hair shorter, faint lines of worry around her mouth that hadn't been there before. She was so small. Somehow that fact registered now more than it ever had — and his need to protect her had never been stronger. Even if she hated him — and how could she not — he still needed to protect her.

"You...you left me, Lake. Why?"

He took another step. "You *know* why. It'll never end for me."

"So why come back?" Her lower lip trembled ever so slightly.

"Because you never left." He stepped closer still, but she held her ground. "Every night, alone in the dark, I remembered. Every night I cursed not having you in my arms, I remembered. The worst thing I've ever done turned out to be the only thing that matters to me anymore."

"You can't just fucking...come back."

For a moment, like the passing of a cloud across the face of the sun, he saw the weight of it, the pain, the loss...and the longing. But was it a longing for what was...or what she hoped would be?

"Yes, I can come back." Lake stood before her, looking down upon the petite beauty who had every reason to hate him, and who'd become the one thing he needed most. "I came back to give you one more choice, Lily girl."

She flinched at the words, but her cheeks colored. God, how he'd missed that blush.

"You don't give me anything anymore, Lake. This is..."

"Tell me to go then. Tell me to leave and never come back to you." He grabbed the hand that held the pistol, wrapping his fingers around hers, raising the gun up again until it pointed at his chest. "Say the words, Lily girl."

Those words were on those sweet, red lips, the lips he could still feel upon his flesh, the lips that spoke her words of devotion, of surrender.

And of love.

But she didn't speak them.

Huge tears welled in those eyes that had haunted him every day they'd been apart.

"I can't..."

"Say it, Lily. Either you say it — or you're mine. For good. Say it, or we find out how deep this goes. Say it — or I'm never letting you go."

Her lips were a deep red O, and he couldn't help but

hold her delicate chin in his hand, stroke those lips with his thumb until, with a sudden intake of breath, she set her forehead to his chest, a deep, hollow sound coming from inside hers.

He slowly lowered her weapon. Popping the magazine from the pistol, he took both from her hand, dropping them to the wood floor, the sound jarring in the small, quiet house. When she quieted, he lifted her face to his, and she pressed a weak fist to his chest, leaning into him as her eyes shut and she wept silently. Lake watched her, watched her release, a profound gratitude flooding through him.

This was right.

For the first time since before the death of his wife, he felt...right.

It didn't matter what forces had brought them together, the lusts, the rage, the twisted desires that drove them both. No, what mattered was this moment. This woman. Forever.

Mine.

She pushed herself away from him, her gaze locked with his, and he knew. They both did. She belonged to him. She was, always...

His.

Without another word, he snaked a hand up to the back of her neck, fingers curling around the base of her skull, his other hand closing over her still-fisted one, holding it to his chest while his mouth closed over hers, pushing her backward until her body pressed against the wall. When her free hand came to his waist, he took it, raising it up over her head, crushing it too, to the wall, his palm flat against hers, fingers intertwining as his kiss deepened, the hunger of too many months without her manifesting in the rough reclaiming of her mouth.

* * *

Passion erupted like nothing else. Lake kissed me hard, but it wasn't enough. I wanted more. I wanted harder. I needed it. I needed everything.

Tearing his mouth from mine, he looked down at me, his breath coming hard, his eyes molten on mine. Gripping my coat, he tore the buttons from it pushing it from me, dropping it to the floor. I reached for his shirt with the same intensity, my fingers clumsy as they worked the buttons while he simply ripped my blouse in half, his mouth once again closing over mine. His hand found one breast and gripped it hard, squeezing it while I pushed his shirt open, my mouth moving to his neck, the scruff along his jaw scratching my face while I sucked on the curve of his shoulder. He turned me, walking me backwards, catching me as I tripped while he stripped off his shirt and led me to the bedroom, pushing me onto the bed, the light of the full moon illuminating us in an almost eerie silvery light.

Opening the buttons of my jeans, he pushed them, along with my panties, down my thighs. I watched him in that light when he did. It was as if he couldn't stop looking at me, even as his gaze had to shift to the work of stripping me. I watched him, my hands reaching for the buckle of his belt, the touch of leather reminding me of the leather he'd used to punish me, the leather I somehow missed. He kissed me again, lifting me higher onto the bed once I was naked, standing for a moment to strip off his pants, his eyes never leaving mine until he could climb on top of me again, his knees nudging mine wider, his cock finding the slick entrance of my ready sex. My breathing came as ragged as his when he gripped my wrists and spread my arms wide, our eyes locking when he thrust deep inside me, causing me to cry out, my body not ready to take him but wanting him all the same, stretching for him. My fingernails dug crevices into my palms as he thrust again and again, harder each time, each stroke punishing, taking, reclaiming, owning.

Finally, he brought his mouth back to mine, our lips opening, not quite kissing, our breath hot, until we both came, the orgasm strange, the sound that came from his chest stranger as he pumped his seed into me, sweat dripping from his forehead onto mine.

Only when he collapsed on top of me did he still, allowing me to cradle him in my arms, some part of me still, even now, even with his cock still inside me, his weight crushing me, his breath hot on my face, in my ear, still not believing that he was here, that he'd come back. That after everything, he'd come back.

I held him for an eternity, neither of us speaking for a long time. Finally, he lifted his head and looked down at me. He slid his cock out of me, my thighs suddenly slick with the gush of his cum on them. Setting his elbows above my shoulders and supporting his weight on his forearms, he kissed me again, that passion somewhat abated, this kiss more tender, slower, more exploratory. And when he pulled back, I saw something in his eyes I'd never seen before. It was a tenderness, but more than that. A strange sort of peace, as if he were, finally, satiated.

"Lake," I said, touching his face, pushing sweat-covered hair from his forehead.

His fingers touched my face in turn, as if he, too, did not believe.

"If you leave again…now…you'll break a piece of me." They were the truest words I'd ever spoken and, in a way, up until now, I'd managed. I'd kept going somehow, but I hadn't been whole, not after the cabin. I hadn't been living. I'd been surviving, that was all.

He touched my face with the tenderest of touches. "I won't break you. Ever. I promise, Lily."

I studied him, my eyes scanning his, and I believed him. And not only that, but I knew in a way that the same was true for him. For the first time since I'd known him, I knew Lake was as fragile, as vulnerable as me. I knew I'd break him as surely as he'd break me. We were the same in this one thing. I believed his promise and I made my own. I had made that long ago though even if I only realized it now.

I smiled when he ran a finger down the bridge of my nose, his touch feather light. "I've missed you, missed everything. I love you, Lily."

I didn't know until hearing them how much those words meant to me. Those words coming from him.

"I love you," I repeated back to him.

He kissed me then, softly, tenderly.

"Make love to me, Lake. Make love to me."

What we'd done now, it wasn't lovemaking. It was fucking; it was hard and it was necessary, the only way for us to come back to each other. Softness didn't suit us, not really, but right now, I needed exactly that. I needed him to make slow love to me, tender love. I needed kisses and caresses and tomorrow I'd take the leather. But not now.

Now, I needed Lake to simply love me.

EPILOGUE

"Lake, my shoulders."

His response was to bring his finger to his lips, telling me without words to be quiet.

That was part of the deal, a part of this exercise.

He checked his watch then leaned back against the wall to watch me, arms folded across his chest, his silence unnerving.

I groaned. He raised an eyebrow in warning and I lowered my gaze to my feet, which were bare, my toes just touching the floor.

We'd stayed off the grid for over a year before finally moving into the secluded house on Graham Island three months ago. The island chain, stretching north of Vancouver Island, was called Haida Gwaii — but Lake still called it the Queen Charlottes. I didn't argue with him.

We meant to settle here. At least I did, anyway. I was finished with hiding, with being on the run and always looking over my shoulder. Although I knew that last part wouldn't ever be over. Not really. We were both too realistic for that.

Randall was locked up, DeSalvo had kept his word — too afraid not to — and it was just Lake and I now. I was ready for more. But first, this little exercise of Lake's.

I watched him, never could get enough of looking at him, his dark eyes, their weighted gaze always drawing me. He stood in worn, faded jeans, his feet bare, his chest naked, the dark trail of hair disappearing into the denim, his erection pressing against his jeans. I licked my lips and gazed up into his eyes once more, lust clouding my vision now. I wanted him, but he wouldn't fuck me. Not yet.

I had a dozen strokes of the crop coming first, after his version of a time out was paid.

I wasn't sure what I disliked more, the lashes themselves, or being strung up in the middle of the barn, naked, dirt beneath my feet, the now familiar scent of horses bringing with it this strange anticipation coupled with unbearable arousal. I did like the fucking though. It was always harder after a whipping, that fucking. And I wanted it every time. Craved it.

Lake checked his watch again, then moved behind me. I would have turned to follow his movements, and could have with the way I was bound, but I knew what was expected of me and remained facing forward, facing the open barn doors, looking at the two horses out in the pasture lazing away the summer afternoon. The sun was bright today, the approaching dark clouds making the light even brighter.

I listened to him, listened to any sign that the cropping was about to begin, but he enjoyed my anticipation too much to make this happen too quickly. My heart beat fast, and it took all my effort not to tense my bottom at the slightest sound. He liked me to keep it soft. Enjoyed watching it bounce and redden with each stroke, and in a way, I liked him watching. I liked giving that to him, that small act of submission.

"Time, Lily," Lake said from behind me, making me

jump.

I nodded, as if my acknowledgment was needed for what came next, the part of this ritual I dreaded and desired all at once.

But we both knew better.

I couldn't help but glance over my shoulder to find him taking the longer crop from the wall. It was the same one he used on Balthazar, his horse — although I was quite certain Balthazar never received the sort of treatment I did with the fearsome implement.

"That's an additional five strokes," he said as he ran his fingers over the crop. He hadn't even turned around.

Shit.

I quickly faced forward once more.

"You know better than that."

He always caught me.

"Five, Lake? Isn't that…"

"Make it six."

I bit my tongue, but stomped my foot.

"Seven then."

I pressed my lips together, forcing myself to remain silent. Nineteen strokes. I could have been done at a dozen.

"Good girl," he said while he lined the crop up against the fleshiest part of my bottom, just inches above the crease of my thighs.

I reached up to wrap my hands around the chain he'd hooked the cuffs to, knowing I'd need the support once he began.

"In silence."

I nodded again, everything completely quiet as if even the sounds of birds and insects from outside no longer penetrated the space. In fact, the only sound was that of the crop as the first stroke came down, the slight whistling a warning before stiff leather struck vulnerable, barely warmed flesh.

I gritted my teeth, clenching everything for a moment

while pain spread across my skin. One down, eighteen to go. At least he didn't make me count today. Today was for his pleasure; it wasn't a punishment I'd earned.

He lined up the second stroke, rubbing the crop across my bottom before pulling back to strike again, just below the first stroke. I stumbled forward, grunting, and before I'd even righted myself, he struck again, three in quick succession, after which it seemed impossible to take the whole of the nineteen strokes in silence.

"Shh," he muttered, his hand on my hip pulling me back a little so that my bottom was pushed out. "Like that. Take the rest like that."

"Yes, Sir."

Calloused fingers traced the line of one of the strokes, crossing over onto another.

"Looks good," he said, stepping back.

I remained as I was, bent slightly, pushing my bottom out, the humiliating position serving to arouse as much as embarrass.

Lake lined up the next stroke at the center of my ass and struck fast, the whipping sound short before pain exploded along the mark. Again, I stumbled but quickly resumed my position for the next stroke, no longer able to keep quiet. He seemed to accept that though and didn't berate me into silence. Instead, he kept up with my punishment, laying stroke after stroke until my nineteen were paid and the whole of my ass throbbed, the flesh hot and tight.

"Stay," he said, although I had no intention of moving. I knew better.

Lake replaced the crop then returned to me. I gasped when his hands wrapped roughly around my hips, thumbs pushing into bruised skin.

"Beautiful," he said, kneeling behind me.

He kissed me first, kissed each of the thin welts the crop had left, his lips tender before he dug his thumbs into the bruised flesh, pulling my cheeks apart. His tongue licked the length of my sex then and he worked two fingers around to find my clit. I gasped, wanting to push back into him but knowing I needed to remain still, to feel everything, every slight movement of his tongue as he licked, his fingers as he worked my hard little nub. I wasn't allowed to come, not yet. He'd only allow it once he'd impaled me on his cock.

"Please, Lake," I said as he continued to tease, to taste.

"Please what?" he asked, rising to stand, letting go of my hips for a moment while he unzipped his jeans.

"Please fuck me. I want to come."

"You want to come?" he asked, lifting me slightly off the ground and pulling me backward so that his length rubbed all along my dripping sex.

I nodded. "Yes. I want to come. I need to come."

"You want me to fuck you hard or soft?"

"You know!" I pressed into him, frustrated at his taunting.

"Say it. I like to hear you say it."

"Fuck me hard, Lake. Fuck me as hard as you whipped me and make me come."

"That's a good girl." He lifted me once more off my feet, this time lowering me onto his cock, making me gasp as he pushed the length of himself hard inside me, my wet pussy needing to stretch to accommodate his girth.

"Yes. Oh yes!" He lifted me slowly, dragging me off his cock before impaling me again, this time closing two fingers over my clit.

"You like being stripped naked and bound while I watch you, Lily?" he asked, lifting again before pulling me hard onto himself. "You like me striping your ass? Because you were dripping before we even started."

"Please..."

He'd need to give permission and I wasn't sure I could stand it. If I didn't though, I'd be in for a real punishment.

"Tell me and I'll let you come, Lily. Tell me how you like it."

I hated that he made me do it. It embarrassed me to no end and he knew it.

At my hesitation, he pulled out of me.

"No!"

"Bad girl." He turned me to face him, lifting me again, taking my arms down, the cuffs off. I wrapped my arms around his neck.

"I'm not a bad girl," I said, kissing him.

"You are." He kissed me back, walking me to where the hay was stacked. "Now I know you don't want that freshly whipped ass to come anywhere near that hay." He kissed me again as I wrapped my legs tightly around his waist. "Tell me. Tell me what you like."

"Please, Lake, you know I hate to say it."

"But I so enjoy making you," he said, his lips never truly leaving mine. "Besides, I won't be able to whip you like this in the coming months." At that he pulled back, smiling, something different in his dark eyes, something almost…happy.

I smiled back, unable not to. I was almost eight weeks pregnant. It hadn't been planned and when I'd first taken the test, I hadn't been sure of Lake's reaction, but it turned out he was even more excited than I was.

We were going to have a baby. The thought of it filled me to overflowing, my happiness so much more than I'd ever imagined possible.

"No, you won't be able to whip me," I said, grinning, teasing, as he set me on my feet. I kissed him again, taking his cock in one hand and massaging its length. "I like it when you watch me, Lake. It makes me drip for you. I like it when you spread me wide and look at me, I like it when you lick me. And I very much like"—slowly, I knelt before him—"taking your cock into my mouth, tasting you." Lake wrapped his fingers into my hair then, groaning as I closed my lips around him, opening my throat for him, taking him deep like he'd taught me.

He looked down at me, his hand in my hair working

now to guide me over his length, pressing deep into my throat while I watched him watching me.

"That's it, girl," he said, his hold tightening, moving me faster, going deeper.

I gripped his thighs, trying to stay relaxed while he fucked my mouth.

"And as much as I want to shoot down your little throat," he said after a while, pulling me off of him and raising me to stand before kissing me once more. "I want something else." He turned me, his breath at my neck as he kissed me, pushing me to bend over the stacked bales of hay. "As much as I like it, I really want to fuck that tight little pussy of yours now."

I bent, stretching my arms wide as he spread my cheeks apart and slid his length into me, causing me to moan.

"So hot and tight," he said. "And that pretty little ass is so nice to watch." He pulled me wider, his thumb coming to press against my bottom hole.

"Please..."

"Come, Lily," he said, "Come on my cock."

He began to fuck me harder then, his breath coming short as he dug his fingers into me, his thumb pressing into my asshole, his cock swelling, the walls of my pussy contracting around it, milking it as I came, forcing a cry from his lips as he stilled, his cock throbbing inside me as he came, filling me.

He wrapped me in a blanket afterwards, just as the first roll of thunder sounded. I watched while he brought the horses back inside, settling them in their stalls, leaving the large doors of the barn open. We sat together quietly watching the storm, tucked safe and warm in the blanket, into Lake's shoulder, his arms around me holding me tight.

"You want a boy or a girl?" I asked, turning my face up to his, nuzzling my chin against the stubble along his jaw.

He smiled, but I knew he also worried. We both did. A child made us vulnerable. Again.

He looked at me. "I want a healthy baby."

Captive, Mine

I smiled, tears warming my eyes.

Lake cupped the back of my head and kissed my forehead, holding his lips there. "I love you, Lily."

I closed my eyes, tears sliding down my face. I laid a hand on his chest, feeling his heart beat beneath my palm.

"I love you, Lake."

THE END

ABOUT THE AUTHORS

Natasha Knight is the author of several BDSM and spanking erotic romances all of which explore the mind of the Dominant male and the submissive female, discovering just beneath the surface of each story that key element of love. Her characters are as human as she: powerful and vulnerable, flawed, perhaps damaged but with an incredible capacity to love.

Trent Evans is an independent author of BDSM erotic romance and erotica. Putting pen to paper since he was a wee lad, he decided to try to share some of the tales cooked up in his fevered imagination. Some readers might not be horrified at what he writes. He tries to write stories that appeal to both women and men (wow, threading the needle), but will follow wherever the story takes him.

A long-time resident of the Pacific Northwest, the author believes that the high percentage of authors in the region (compared to the nation as a whole) is chiefly due to the fact that it's so damned wet and miserable all the time there. They tend to use their long hours cooped up inside spinning yarns that depict things they'll never see or experience — such as sunshine.

Printed in Great Britain
by Amazon.co.uk, Ltd.,
Marston Gate.